CONNECTED TO THE PLUG

DWAN WILLIAMS

Date: 12/5/18

Good2Go Publishing

CONNECTED TO THE PLUG 4
Written by Dwan Williams
Cover Design: Davida Baldwin
Typesetter: Mychea
ISBN: 9781947340237
Copyright © 2018 Good2Go Publishing
Published 2018 by Good2Go Publishing
7311 W. Glass Lane • Laveen, AZ 85339
www.good2gopublishing.com
https://twitter.com/good2gobooks
G2G@good2gopublishing.com
www.facebook.com/good2gopublishing
www.instagram.com/good2gopublishing

DEDICATION

This book, just like many others, is dedicated to my great-grandmother, Georgiana "Granny Wanny" Williams-Barnes and all of my fans/followers. Also to my family that has shown me their support through all this. I love you all.

ACKNOWLEDGMENTS

I would like to acknowledge J. Wheeler, Partee, Fred Cloud, Jack Rabbit, and everyone else out there that has supported me and shown love by purchasing my books.

I would also like to acknowledge a few friends behind the walls, whether state or federal: my big bruh Carlton "Brontae" May, Chris Murray, Jasper "J-Mudd" Allen, Jerry Mercer, Demeco "5" Richardson, Louis Garcia, Yahshua, and last but definitely not least, Kimberly Floyd for constantly inspiring me to continue striving in my journey. For those of you who I didn't mention, FORGIVE ME!

I would like to acknowledge Good2Go for giving me this platform to share my work with each and every one of you. Also, Shonda Gray for her time and effort in the research of this project and many others.

Peace & Blessings

1

After Hadji got dressed, he found his way downstairs. "Damn, this shit is big as hell," he said to himself as he walked down the long hallway toward the front door. To Hadji, it was like everything started to move in slow motion. Once he made it to the double doors and pulled them open, his heart dropped and his mouth fell wide open in shock. Sherry stood before him with tears running down her face and a heart full of pain. What shocked him the most was when he saw the gun he purchased for her a few years ago. He knew she was well aware of how to use it because he took her to target practice for months.

He had no idea how he was going to explain the predicament he found himself in, but he damn sure was about to try. "I-I-I," he began to stutter, but Sherry raised her hand to silence him. CLICK-CLACK!

"You promised me you would never hurt me, Hadji," Sherry cried as tears freely trailed down her face. Her lips quivered and Hadji could see the hurt and pain in her eyes, but what frightened him the most was the hate he saw dead within them. He had seen firsthand what a woman scorned could be capable of. Hadji knew he had to think quick before Sherry's shaking finger accidentally pulled back on the trigger.

"Baby, please lower the gun before you make a mistake and shoot me," he pleaded in a calm voice. He was very cautious not to upset her any more than she already was. He could see the wheels turning in her head and held his hands in the air to show her he was not a possible threat. Once he felt he had things under control, Hadji took a step closer—which he would regret. POW! A single shot blasted through the air and ripped into his chest, making him pause in his steps. "YOU SHOT ME!" Hadji gasped, surprised as he fell to one knee and gripped his chest. With all the bad things Hadji had done in his life, he knew death was inevitable, but never in a million years would he have ever imagined he would have been taken out by the one person he loved more than life itself.

Hadji fell forward and hit the ground face-first with a loud thud. "I-I-I-I love y-y-you, Sherry," he coughed through bloody lips, right before Sherry became a blur and he heard another thunderous gunshot cut through the air before everything went black.

~ ~ ~

As soon as Fuzzy entered through the sliding doors of the Wilson Memorial Hospital emergency room entrance, she was greeted by Slim and the rest of the crew/family. Everyone watched her run across the lobby into her uncle's awaiting arms. No one dared to speak as she laid her head on his chest to cry her heart out. It was no secret to Slim or anyone there how Fuzzy felt about Hadji. Slim held his niece tightly in his embrace, wishing he could take away her pain. "Everything is going to be alright," he promised her, then kissed the top of her head while rubbing his hand on her back in a circular motion. Fuzzy knew she had to pull herself together in front of the family because she didn't want to appear weak. Fuzzy sniffled away her tears, wiped her eyes, and then held her head up high. When she looked around the room, she was shocked at what she saw. Not only were there people she didn't even know in tears, but also even the most rugged and thorough thugs in the crew/family tried their best to mask the hurt and pain for their fallen general.

Just as the doctor walked into the lobby with his report, the sliding door to the emergency room slid open and in walked an unfamiliar face. "Who is here for a Mr. and Mrs. Clark?" the doctor questioned as he scanned the room for their next of kin.

"I am," the unfamiliar face and Fuzzy spoke at the same time. Dr. Turner looked over his small wire-framed glasses at the two women before him, trying to figure out who to give the update to.

"Well, my name is Mya Ingram and I am here on behalf of Mrs. Clark," the unfamiliar face walked up to the doctor and responded. "I am her sister." Mya watched as the doctor began to turn the pages on his clipboard until he found the page he was looking for.

"Ah, here we go. Mrs. Sherry Clark," Dr. Turner began. "I'm sorry to inform you that your sister has a self-inflicted wound to her head, it says here. She is listed in critical condition at this time." Mya stood in front of Dr. Turner in disbelief at the news he had just dropped on her. Never in a million years would she believe that Sherry would try to take her own life. "I was also told that Mrs. Clark will not be allowed to have any visitors if she wakes up." Now Mya was really confused.

"And why is that?" she wanted to know. Dr. Turner looked to Mya and then to Fuzzy and the rest of the crew before answering.

"One of the officers said the bullet that shot Mr. Clark is the same exact kind of bullet that shot Mrs. Clark."

"Okay, but I am also Mrs. Clark's attorney," Mya

announced. She pulled out her business card and handed it to the doctor before turning around and walking over to the far side of the lobby and taking a seat. As Dr. Turner looked over Mya's credentials, Fuzzy walked up on him. "And what about Mr. Clark? Is he going to be alright?" She knew Hadji had been shot in the chest, so she just wanted to know how bad his injury actually was.

"Oh, yes, Mr. Clark," Dr. Turner repeated as he flipped back through the papers on his clipboard. "Mr. Clark took a bullet to the chest." Everyone watched as the doctor's brow raised. "Another inch to the left and it would have hit his heart." He went on to explain how lucky Hadji was to still be living. "He's heavily medicated right now," Dr. Turner informed the crew, and then looked at his watch. "But, if y'all want to see him before the officers come back to question him, y'all have about thirty minutes."

"Thank you, Bennie." Slim smiled and shook his long-time friend's hand, slipping a few hundred-dollar bills into his palm. To his surprise, when Dr. Turner released his hand, the money was still in it.

"I know he's family, so your money is no good with me right now," Dr. Turner assured him. He gave Slim Hadji's room number and then disappeared through the double sliding doors of the emergency room lobby. Fuzzy was the last to follow Slim out of the lobby. She stopped short at the doorway and turned to take one last look at Mya. She made a mental note to find out as much as she could about the woman claiming to be Sherry's sister. Little did she know, Mya knew more about her than she could ever imagine.

~ ~ ~

Hadji slept for two days straight before he finally began to come to. Within those two days, two detectives by the name of Tisdale and Meeks stopped by every few hours to see if they could catch him awake so they could get a lead on their case. On one of their visits, Mya happened to stop in to check on him and warned them that she was his lawyer and when he came around, she would have him get in contact with them to answer any questions concerning the shooting. They took the card and hadn't been back since. That was good with Fuzzy because she knew if they knew it was her house they got shot at, they would probably still be questioning her. That was something she was not up for at the time.

Fuzzy had been by Hadji's side day and night watching over him. Slim ordered Jamontae and Diontae to stay behind also to watch over him to make sure whomever wanted him dead didn't come back and finish the job. However, Fuzzy assured them she had that part covered and sent them to Sherry's room to keep an eye out for her just in case anyone came to do her any harm. After assuring them Hadji would appreciate that more than anything, they went and took their post. They figured if they did that job correctly, Hadji would most definitely promote them up the food chain when he fully recovered.

"What happened?" Hadji asked after adjusting his eyes to the light in the room. He had no idea where he was, but when he tried to sit up, a sharp pain in his chest shot to the rest of his upper body making him tense up and squeeze Fuzzy's hand. Fuzzy opened her eyes when she felt his tight grip.

"You're awake." She smiled then sat up in her chair she was resting in beside his bed. Hadji's sight had not quite adjusted and he could barely make out her voice.

"Sherry!" he called out, hoping his wife was the first face he saw. Fuzzy's smile slowly disappeared.

"It's me, Hadji, Fuzzy." She waited a few seconds for him to reply, but he didn't. He drifted off back to sleep. For the next few hours, Hadji tossed and turned in his sleep in what Fuzzy guessed was a nightmare because he would occasionally moan a couple of words, jump, or turn his head from side to side. Several times, Fuzzy had to wipe sweat from his head and brow as he slept. She talked to him most of the time she was awake. That seemed to calm him, and she was happy about that. Before long, Hadji was in a comatose-like state until the following day.

~ ~ ~

Mya stayed by Sherry's side, only leaving to go get food since she came prepared with spare clothes and her briefcase filled with the legal work of her clients. Every now and then, Jamontae and Diontae would come into the room and check on Sherry or see if Mya needed anything. She thought that was nice of them, even though she knew they were only following orders. "Come on, Sherry. I need you to wake up for me and tell me what happened. I know you didn't shoot Hadji. You love his ass too damn much to do that." She smiled thinking about all they had been through over the years. "I especially know you would never try to take your own life." She knew Sherry was what people called "a true religious person." She was very old-fashioned and though she loved Hadji more than life itself, she made him wait until they were married to have sex with her. Mya knew that sooner or later, Sherry would give her some kind of sign. She just prayed it would be sooner than later.

8

~ ~ ~

When Fuzzy walked out of the bathroom, she noticed Hadji was wide awake staring at the ceiling as if he was in deep thought. "Nice for you to join us. You gave us quite a scare." She made her way back across the room to her chair posted up beside his bed. Due to the fact that Hadji had limited memory of why he was in the hospital, he had a lot of questions he needed answered.

"Fuzzy," he called out to her after a few more minutes of silence. "Is she dead?" He watched her take a seat beside his bed and waited patiently for her to answer.

"Hadji," Fuzzy began and then placed her hand on his, "Sherry isn't doing too well." She let her words sink in before continuing. "After she shot you, she tried to take her own life." Hadji closed his eyes tightly and said a silent prayer for his wife.

"What have I done?" he asked himself just above a whisper. Fuzzy watched a few tears trail down his face before leaning over and wiping them for him. "Uncle Slim got Jamontae and Diontae on her door to watch over her until you get better." She was hoping that little bit of news would lighten the load on Hadji's shoulders. There was one question Hadji wanted to know the answer to. He had asked himself the question at least a thousand times since he had been lying in the hospital.

"Fuzzy." He opened his eyes and looked in her direction.

"Yes?"

"Did we have sex that night?" Hadji didn't remember much, but he did remember waking up in her bed with only his boxers on. Just as she was about to answer, Dr. Turner came into the room holding his clipboard.

"Good morning, Mr. Clark. How are you feeling this morning?"

Hadji looked at Dr. Turner with an expression on his face that said, "Do I really need to answer that question?" Dr. Turner caught on to the look Hadji gave him and began flipping through the pages on his clipboard. "I have some good news that will lift your spirits," Dr. Turner announced when he found the paper he was looking for.

"What? This is all a bad dream and you're about to wake me up?" Hadji asked sarcastically. Ignoring Hadji's last comment, Dr. Turner gave him the good news.

"Your wife woke up this morning." Hadji looked into the doctor's eyes to see if he was serious because Hadji was not in a joking mood. "She asked for you." Hadji tried to sit up too fast, and the pain he felt in his chest was like being hit with a 30,000-watt volt of electricity from a taser. "Mr. Clark, relax. Two male nurses are on the way with a wheelchair, and they will take you to her room." Dr. Turner looked at Fuzzy and acknowledged her before making his exit from the room. By the time Hadji's pain began to subside, the two nurses were helping him into the wheelchair. Once he was secure, they left Fuzzy to wheel him to Sherry's room.

When Fuzzy wheeled Hadji into Sherry's room, she and Mya were sound asleep. "What's up Cuzo?" Hadji greeted Mya when Fuzzy wheeled his chair next to her, nudging her leg. Mya opened her eyes slowly.

"Hadji?" she questioned, thinking she was still asleep. When she looked up and saw Fuzzy behind him, she knew she wasn't dreaming. If she was, it was a nightmare.

"How is she?" he asked, his voice filled with concern.

"She's strong, that's for sure," Mya replied with a weak smile. "She woke up earlier asking for you." It hurt him knowing he wasn't there when she needed him.

"Hadji," Sherry called out when she heard his voice. Hadji turned his head in her direction. Her eyes were still closed, but she had her arm out to her side with her hand open waiting for him to put his hand in it. Fuzzy wheeled Hadji over to Sherry's bedside and watched him hold her hand. She tried to hold the fake smile she had on her face, because she could feel Mya staring a hole in the side of her face, but Mya could see the jealousy in her eyes. She was very good at spotting things like that in her profession, amongst other things. "I'm sorry, Hadji," Sherry apologized. "I—," Sherry began, but Hadji stopped her.

"Shhh. Save your energy, babe." Sherry felt a lone tear fall from Hadji's eyes onto her hand. When she looked over at her husband, she too began to cry. When she noticed Fuzzy staring down at them, her tears of love turned into tears of anger which made her snatch her hand from Hadji's. Shocked, Hadji looked up into Sherry's eyes. She stared at Fuzzy menacingly.

"What the fuck is she doing here, Hadji?" He tried to find the words, but none came out. "Get out," she shouted. "Both of you!" Hadji looked from Sherry to Fuzzy and then to Mya for help. "Leave," she demanded. Before she could get another word out, a surging pain shot to her head. "Ahhh." She tensed up before going limp.

"Sherrrryyyy!" Hadji shouted. He tried to get out of his wheelchair to help her, but fell to the floor in his attempt. Sherry's monitor got weaker until finally it flatlined.

"Everyone get out!" Dr. Turner demanded when he

entered the room. The two nurses that helped Hadji into the wheelchair came in and helped him off the floor. Hadji took one last look at his wife before he was forced to leave her once again.

~ ~ ~

Hadji stayed in the hospital for another week before he was released. He tried to go see Sherry several times while he was there, but she refused to see him. Mya talked Hadji into giving Sherry a little time to herself, so he did just that. "You ready?" Fuzzy asked as Hadji stood outside of Sherry's room watching her sleep through the small window of her door.

"Yeah," Hadji replied. Fuzzy headed down the hall to give Hadji a little privacy. After a few minutes had passed, Hadji made his way out of the hospital, where Fuzzy was out front waiting to take him home.

The ride to Knightdale was made in complete silence. Well, besides the soft sound of Floetry groaning through the speakers. They were both lost in their own thoughts until the GPS interrupted. "Make a left in .1 miles, and your destination will be straight ahead," it informed them. A couple of seconds later, Fuzzy was making a left onto Hadji's block. To her surprise, his place was the only one at the dead end of the cul-de-sac. Fuzzy had to admit she was quite impressed. It wasn't as big as the mansion she and Speedy shared, but it was larger than average. She estimated it had to be sitting on at least five or more acres of well-manicured land. As they approached, Hadji fished his keys out of his jacket and pressed the button on his keychain. Immediately the gates slid apart and gave Fuzzy entrance to the property. "Thanks for the ride," Hadji said right before Fuzzy got the chance to hit the start button to kill the engine.

"No problem." She smiled. She watched Hadji walk up the set of stairs that led to the front door. Once she made sure he was safely inside, she backed out of the driveway, called Sheila, and let her know she was on her way to pick up Sade and Lil Menace. Hadji watched Fuzzy pull off his estate from his living room window. When she was out of sight, he walked over to his fully stacked bar and fixed himself a drink. He had a lot of things to try to figure out, and as soon as he got himself back on track physically, as well as mentally, he was going to get down to the bottom of who was behind the attempt on his life. Since they had involved his wife, Hadji was now declaring a war, and the city of Wilson was about to feel his wrath.

2

Tawana sat straight up in her bed in a cold sweat, just as she had done every night for the past few weeks since she had returned to New Jersey with her son Junior. No matter what she did, she couldn't shake the dream of someone taking him away from her again. Tawana vowed she would give her life before she let that happen again.

Just like every other night after she awoke, Tawana grabbed her pistol from under her pillow, slid her feet into her slippers, and then walked across her bedroom to cover her nakedness with her silk robe on the back of the chair at her desk. Once she entered the long hallway and reached the other end where Junior's room sat, she couldn't do anything but smile as she approached his door. Since she always kept it cracked, it made it easy for her to peep her head in to check on Junior without waking him. "Junior," she called out with a voice full of worry. She loaded a round in the chamber when she noticed Junior wasn't in his bed. Tawana entered the room with caution and then searched under his bed. Finding nothing but a couple of toys and a few cookie wrappers under it, she stood to her feet and headed for the closet. When she reached for the door handle to slide it back, she heard a noise downstairs. Her greatest fears were coming to life, and to make matters worse, the intruders were still in the house. Tawana scaled the stairs quietly, careful not to warn her surprise guest that she was nearing. With her gun held high, ready to give it to whoever wanted it, she stood wide legged in the center of the doorway to the kitchen. "Junior." She breathed a sigh of relief then lowered her weapon to her side. She didn't even bother to try to conceal it. Besides, she had nowhere to hide it since all she had on was her silk robe. "What are you doing standing on that chair?" she asked already knowing the answer. Although Junior smiled, it was not because he was happy, it was because he had gotten caught in the act of trying to grab the bag of Soft Batch cookies from the top shelf of the pantry. "Let me help you with that." She smiled as she made her way across the kitchen to assist him with his mission. Junior hopped down from the chair and slid it back to its rightful spot at the table and then took a seat.

Once Tawana grabbed the cookies, she walked over to the fridge and pulled out the gallon of milk before retrieving two glasses and then sitting down beside her son. Within five minutes, they had both finished the bag of cookies and downed two glasses of milk.

After they were done with their late-night snack,

Tawana led the way back upstairs. "Can I sleep with you tonight, Mommy?" Junior asked, surprising Tawana.

"Of course, you can," Tawana replied. Little did Junior know, she was more than happy to let him sleep with her. Maybe then the nightmares would go away, at least that's what she hoped. Once they were situated in her bed, Tawana looked at the time. "Three o'clock," she said to herself, then picked up her cell and texted her sister, Crystal. "Don't forget about tomorrow," she typed, and then sent the message. She knew not to wait up for a reply because she knew one would never come. Instead, she held Junior tightly, closed her eyes, and fell into a deep sleep.

~ ~ ~

Tawana found herself staring glassy-eyed with a big smile on her face as she watched Junior resting peacefully beside her. She ran her manicured nails through his thick hair as he snored lightly. She reminisced of the times she and his father, Speedy, used to share, back when they were the perfect pair. Back to the time when she was the Bonnie to his Clyde. That thought was short lived when she looked at her Cartier and saw the time. She knew things couldn't be put off any longer and she couldn't be late, not even a minute. After leaning over and planting a kiss on Junior's forehead, Tawana quietly eased out of bed, careful not to wake him. Once her feet were on the floor, she slid them into her slippers and then headed to the bathroom to get herself together.

"Good morning, Ms. Deloris," Tawana greeted as she entered the kitchen.

Deloris was someone that came highly recommended to Tawana's late boyfriend, King, before his demise. From her first day on the job, King knew he was going to keep her around. Not because she was attractive to him, because he didn't look at her in that kind of light. It was because she reminded him of his late mother. On top of that, Deloris was a great cook and gave him the best advice, in and out of the streets. It was rumored that she was a queenpin in her day.

"Good morning, Mrs. King," Deloris replied as she walked over to the table and sat the tray she had in her hand on top of it. Tawana sat down in her favorite seat, which used to be King's seat, at the head of the table, and looked down at the english muffin and jar of strawberry preserves resting beside a steaming cup of coffee.

"Mmmm," Tawana moaned as she took a sip of coffee and then set it down in front of her. "How many times do I have to tell you it's okay to call me Tawana?" she asked, cutting her eyes in Ms. Deloris's direction. Instead of responding, Ms. Deloris waved her off and then headed out of the kitchen. Tawana's eyes followed her, and within a few seconds, Ms. Deloris reappeared with the morning paper in her hand.

"What is this world coming to?" Ms. Deloris asked. She then set the newspaper in front of Tawana, not intending to answer the question Tawana had asked before she exited the kitchen. Tawana knew waiting for an answer to her question was a waste of time, so she picked the paper up and read the headlines. "The crime rate has reached an all-time high in the capital city of New Jersey (TRENTON)," she read. "This city used to be organized back when I was in them streets," Deloris continued. Tawana loved when Deloris ranted on about "back in the day" when she and her late husband ran the streets, but right now she was a little pressed for time, so that would have to wait until a later date.

"Umm, Ms. Deloris, was Crystal home when you got up this morning?"

"Yes, my dear. She wanted me to make sure you were up and ready this morning, but as we can see, up and ready you are." She smiled her warm, loving smile then poured herself a cup of coffee from her favorite mug that read "SUPER WOMAN," that King had had specially made for her. Tawana looked down at her Cartier watch, took one last bite of her muffin, and then chased it with a sip of her coffee.

"Well, I have to be going." Tawana stood to her feet. "Make sure Junior eats all of his food and have him dressed in an hour for me, please." Tawana folded the newspaper and placed it under her arm and then grabbed her handbag.

"Okay, no problem, Mrs. King," Deloris replied and then stood to her feet and began removing the items Tawana left on the table and putting them on a tray. Tawana stopped in her tracks and looked over her shoulder. "Go on 'head now before you be late, chile," Ms. Deloris warned, giving Tawana her back to place the dishes in the dishwasher. Tawana shook her head from side to side, grateful that Ms. Deloris decided to stay around after King's death. Her wisdom was much needed and appreciated. Ms. Deloris smiled to herself as she heard Tawana's departing footsteps.

Tawana stepped outside of the double doors to the mansion, and the rays from the sunlight almost blinded her. She grabbed her Chanel frames from the matching handbag and slid them onto her face. "Good morning, Bo," Tawana greeted her driver and bodyguard as she made her way down the steps to her awaiting Bentley truck.

Bo was a six-foot-seven burly looking figure with a scar that ran down the right side of his face that intimidated most people that came in contact with him. But to Tawana, Crystal, and Ms. Deloris, he was their gentle giant. Tawana was grateful when Deloris and Bo agreed to move into the extra guest rooms of the massive estate.

"Good morning, B.B.," Bo spoke as he removed his Ray-Ban sunglasses from his sweaty face. He stood with the back door of the truck open, waiting for her to get in. When she was securely in the vehicle, Bo shut the door behind her, looked around for anything out of the ordinary, and then made his way to the driver side. Once Bo was inside, he pressed the Start button and brought the engine of the luxury truck to life.

~ ~ ~

Bo pulled the truck in front of Dee-Dee's bar on Brunswick Avenue and killed the engine. After hopping out and checking his surroundings, he made his way around to the back passenger door and opened it. He rested his hand on his pistol with one hand and helped Tawana exit with the other.

Tawana and Bo walked into the bar and took a seat, as they did every time they visited the establishment. There was always a handful of patrons in the place each time they came. Tawana figured her connect kept it that way so things would seem normal to the unexpecting eyes that happened to come in at that time of day. "Follow me, please," a female voice spoke from behind them. Without speaking, Tawana and Bo followed the curvy female to the set of stairs on the other side of the bar, that led to the basement.

When they reached the bottom of the stairs, the woman went to her spot behind the bar as two armed men came to pat Tawana and Bo down—well, Bo, that is, since Tawana was wearing a see-through Chanel sundress. They did search her handbag, though. "Tawana," a low voice called her name from the dimly lit booth in the far corner of the room. Tawana made her way in that direction, but halted when she heard words being exchanged between Bo and the two men that searched him.

"It's okay, Bo. I'm good." Bo nodded, then slapped one of the men's hand that had placed it on his chest to stop him from walking across the room with Tawana.

"One day!" Bo threatened both of the men.

"One day!" one of the men said back, holding Bo's stare while the other huffed and then blew him a kiss challenging him to make the first move. If it was under any other circumstances, Bo would have broken the first man's nose and gone toe-to-toe with the other one, but he had no intentions of messing up the business they had come for.

"I'm glad you could make it. You look absolutely beautiful," Tamar complimented while standing to his feet and extending his hand to Tawana.

Tamar was around six feet even, with brown skin and

a muscular physique. With his boyish face and deep dimples, one would never imagine he ran a huge part of Trenton's drug trade. As a matter of fact, he had his hands in a majority of the cities as far east as Atlantic City. That's where he and King first met. Actually he had his eyes set on Tawana, but after a few lucky hands at the crap table and a lengthy conversation over dinner, King and Tamar found out they had a lot in common. Out of respect for King, Tamar never pursued Tawana and kept doing business with her after he was killed. She made it harder every time she came to do business, being that she rarely kept herself covered.

Once Tawana placed her hand in his, Tamar brought it up to his lips and kissed the back of it. Tawana had to admit to herself that he was definitely someone she could see herself with if they had met under different circumstances, but they had not, so she removed her hand from his and then took her seat across from him and set her handbag on the floor.

"Thank you." She blushed. "You know I always answer when the streets call on me," she replied matter of factly. Tamar nodded his head in agreement and then took his seat.

"So, tell me, how was your trip down South?" Tamar asked, making small talk.

"It was fine," Tawana answered, ready to get to the

business at hand. Tamar's phone buzzed on his hip, so he picked it up and read the text that was waiting on him. When he placed it back on his hip, Tamar clapped his hands twice, and the woman at the bar came from behind it. All eyes were on her until she exited the room. Bo cringed because it was times like these he hated being without his gun. Two minutes later, the woman re-entered the room carrying a handbag identical to the one Tawana had set on the floor beside her.

"Well, I hate to be rude, but I have other business to attend to," Tamar announced and rounded the table to help assist Tawana to her feet. Tawana took his hand and then turned to the female that approached her.

"Thank you," she told the woman that handed her the bag she was carrying. Without responding, the woman turned on her heels and took her position back behind the bar. "Bitch," Tawana mumbled under her breath and then turned back to Tamar, who stood with a smile on his face. She figured the woman and Tamar had to be messing around. "You see, that's why I don't mix business with pleasure." Tawana rolled her eyes and then headed for the door. Tamar watched her backside sway from side to side in admiration.

"Damn! I gotta make her mine," he said to himself as his bodyguard gave Bo back his gun and then escorted them out of the room.

"I don't like them clown-ass niggas," Bo admitted on their way back upstairs to the bar area.

"They were just doing their jobs." Tawana waved him off. They entered the bar area and took a seat on the stool in front of the bar. Tawana placed her small hand on Bo's big broad shoulder and gave it a light squeeze. She knew Bo was overprotective of her; that's why she kept him near at all times.

As they sipped on the drinks they had ordered and made small talk, they got interrupted by a loud and rowdy couple that came into the bar. "So why was that bitch all up in yo' damn face, Kevin?" the chick asked as they approached the bar.

"Man, go 'head with that bullshit, Laquita." Kevin held his hand up as he took a seat two stools over from Tawana as Laquita took it upon herself to sit on the stool between Tawana and her man Kevin. Tawana shook her head and laughed at the couple. Even though the chick was a little rough around the edges, Tawana could tell she had a lot of style, because she carried the same exact handbag she had, and it wasn't cheap.

"Man, go 'head my ass," Laquita went on.

"Can I please get a double shot of Hennessy?" Kevin ordered, rubbing his low-cut Caesar. Bo shook his head at the poor guy, knowing his woman had to be a handful.

"Make that two doubles," Laquita corrected.

25

"Because he gonna need it." The bartender smiled and then made his way to the other end of the bar to fix the drinks. When he returned, Kevin took the first shot and downed it in one swallow. He let the burn settle in before he reached for the second glass, but he was a second too slow. Laquita had already picked it up and downed it. That just started up another argument. That was Tawana and Bo's cue to go. After paying their tab, they headed for the door. Tawana looked back one last time at the couple and couldn't do anything but laugh. Bo just shook his head and then escorted Tawana back to the truck.

Bo was a few blocks from the bar when he looked into the rearview mirror and noticed they were being followed. "We got company, B.B.," he stated calmly. He put the truck in neutral, turned the radio off then back on, and then watched the secret compartment slide out from the center console. Once Bo secured his gun, he did the exact same method in reverse and then watched the gun disappear. Bo had put the truck back in drive by the time the unmarked police cruiser put on his flashing lights. Bo slowly pulled the truck over to the curb. He watched with caution as the plainclothes officer exited his vehicle with his hand hovering over his service pistol. "Is there a problem, Officer?" Bo asked once the window was halfway down. Bo knew the officer was more than likely trying to see who occupied the vehicle, because he was sure not to break any traffic laws.

"License and registration please, sir," the officer demanded. Bo shook his head as he lifted his arm. "Slowly," the officer cautioned him. It was at that very moment that Bo hated the decision he made to hide his gun. Being unarmed and shot by the police was the last way he wanted to go out. Bo retrieved his license and registration card from over the sun visor and then handed it to the officer.

"What was the problem again, Officer?" Bo asked again.

"It's Detective Bass, not Officer," he corrected. "I received a domestic call on a couple arguing a few blocks back and was told they had entered Dee-Dee's. When I parked, I noticed you two exiting the building," Detective Bass answered after looking over Bo's information and handing it back to him. "Have you been drinking, sir?" Before Bo could answer, Tawana spoke up from the backseat.

"We only had one drink, Detective." Tawana leaned up, speaking for the first time since the stop. Detective Bass looked in the backseat to get a good look at the woman he saw exit the bar with the driver. "Damn," he cursed when he noticed Tawana's thick brown thighs her sundress did little to conceal. "And what is your name?" he asked, trying to remember her face.

"Tawana," she answered with a flirtatious smile on her face, one that did not go unnoticed by the thirsty detective.

"Well, Ms. Tawana, since you two have been drinking, would y'all mind stepping out of the truck for me and taking a breathalyzer?" the detective asked. He knew they were not drunk. He really just wanted to see what Tawana looked like close up, outside of the truck.

"Sure, Detective," she agreed, ready to get the stop over with. She was ready to get home to spend time with her son, and the nosey detective was holding her up. Bo and Tawana stepped out of the truck, and as luck would have it, a gust of wind came out of nowhere and lifted Tawana's skirt up, almost exposing her shaven goodies. She giggled when she caught the detective staring. "I need to pat you down for my safety," Bass told Bo. As he patted Bo down, Detective Bass kept his eyes on Tawana, hoping another gust of wind would blow. After he was sure Bo was clean, he walked over to Tawana.

"You want to search me too?" she smiled with her hands high in the air. Detective Bass knew he couldn't search her person, and he really didn't want to call in for back-up since he had no real reason for stopping them in the first place. Besides that, he was unofficially staking out the well-known bar, so he opted just to search the handbag she had on her shoulder. Coming up empty,

Detective Bass let them go on their way. Before he did though, Tawana dug in her handbag and then handed him her business card.

"The Queen's Palace," he read. "It can't be," he thought. "I knew I remembered her from somewhere." He thumped the back of the card as Bo escorted her into the back of the truck. Detective Bass had been investigating King before his death. No matter how close he thought he came to busting King, he would somehow miraculously escape him. As soon as Bo pulled off, Tawana called Tamar and told him about the encounter.

~ ~ ~

Crystal and Ant walked into the old house Crystal purchased when she first moved to New Jersey. It was the one King was killed in, the one Lil Man spared her and Tawana's life in a few years ago. Even though she and Tawana lived together now, she kept it as a stash house that they packaged and stored their drugs at. "Yo, we played that shit off like pros," Ant boasted as he took a seat on the couch in the front room. Crystal knew they did, but was pissed at him.

"Nigga, if you put your hands on my ass one more time, you're gonna lose your fingers," she promised on her way through the living room to the kitchen. Halfway through, Crystal decided to put a little extra sway in her hips, knowing that Ant was looking at her ass. She loved to play with Ant like that, and even though he was cute to her, she wouldn't take things there with him.

"Come on, Crys. Lighten up, damn. I had to make that shit look official."

"You heard what the fuck I said," Crystal finalized. She then went into the kitchen cabinets to get the utensils to begin breaking the work down. This was the part of the job Ant hated, cooking up the work.

Once Crystal successfully cut the bricks of powder with the baking powder, she recompressed and neatly packaged them back up and then stamped them. She was getting off her cell with her Virginia clientel when Ant finished cooking and weighing the last brick of crack. "We'll meet you at the strip club in a few days," Crystal assured him as she threw her handbag on her shoulder.

"That's a bet," Ant shouted. He then glanced over his shoulder to get one last look at Crystal's backside. After Ant placed the work in his duffle bag, he made sure everything was cleaned up, and then headed out the back door to start his mission. Even though money was on his mind as he backed out of the fence that surrounded the house, Crystal stayed front and center in his thoughts.

~ ~ ~

Ant sat at the light on the corner of Brunswick and Olden Avenue, after dropping off the money he had picked up from their spots. He was trying to figure out what type of food he was in the mood for. "Bingo," he said to himself when it hit him. He made a quick right on Olden Avenue, and within a minute flat, he was jumping on Route 1 heading south. "Trenton Makes and the World Takes," he read the big red letters on the bridge adjacent to his right. After riding a ways down, Ant merged on to I-95.

Within thirty minutes, Ant was taking Exit 22 into Center City in Philadelphia. He inhaled the stale air and smiled. "Ahhh." He exhaled, remembering the first time he actually entered the City of Brotherly Love with Crystal a few weeks ago after one of their many pickups. Ant cruised down South Street, taking in all of the sights. It was much different from the slow country life he was used to down South. People were out everywhere. All shapes, colors, and sizes, getting their hustle on. "There we go," he grinned. He then pulled his Range Rover to the curb in front of Jim's Steak and parked behind a money-green 5 Series BMW. "Chelsea," he read the New Jersey license plate.

Jim's was well known in Philly as well as the surrounding cities and states for their Philly cheese steaks, amongst other foods. Its small black and white structure sat on the corner of South and Lombard Street not too far from Temple University. That was also one of the main reasons Ant enjoyed frequenting the small corner store.

After making sure his gun was cocked and loaded, Ant secured it inside of his waistband, jumped out of his truck, and then bopped his way into the building. "Wassup, Jim," Ant greeted the man he'd come to know as the owner.

"My man." Jim looked up and smiled. "How can I help you today?" Jim wiped his hand on the apron in front of him and then reached his hand out to Ant. They had become really cool with each other over the past month, since Ant visited the establishment at least twice a week if not more. Before Ant could place his order, the hooded customer at the counter spoke up.

"I believe I was here first," a female voice announced, sliding the hood from over her head and looking in his direction. By the look on her face, Ant could tell she was pissed.

"My bad, lil mama," Ant apologized. He then gestured for her to place her order. After rolling her eyes, Chelsea did just that. Her jazzy attitude made him think of the females back home. She kind of put him in the mind of the chick Keisha from the movie *Belly*. He stood back and took in her slim and petite frame through her fitted Dior jogging suit. He could tell she wasn't an around-the-way hood rat he had run across since he moved upstate, noticing her ears, neck, and hands full of diamonds. He looked back at the BMW parked outside and stepped out on a limb once Jim returned with both of their orders.

"That will be $10.75," he announced, placing the hooded female's order on the counter. Before she got the chance to go into her handbag to pay for her order, Ant intervened.

"I got this, Jim." Ant went into his pocket, pulled out his knot, and then handed a fifty-dollar bill to Jim. The girl was about to protest, until Ant insisted. "It's not up for dispute." He smiled and then reached over and grabbed his bag from the counter. She watched as he walked toward the door.

"Your change, my friend," Jim called out. Ant turned around insulted. For the short time he had been coming to the store, he never, not even once accepted his change from Jim. "Thank you." Jim waved gracefully and then slid the money back into the register.

By the time Ant started his truck, the female was making her way out of the store. "Chelsea," he called out with his head out the window. Chelsea kept walking and opened up the door to her Beamer. After he called out to her again, Chelsea slid her food over to the passenger's seat and then stood up. Ant's stomach began to flutter watching her make her way over to him. It was something about the way she walked that made him have to have her.

"How do you know my name?" she asked nervously

with her hands inside her hoodie. Her stare was daring, and though her voice sounded nervous, it was also deadly.

"Whoa, shorty. Your name is on your license plate." He pointed to her custom-made New Jersey tag. Chelsea looked at her license plate and then relaxed. She had done so much dirt in her past, she didn't know if Ant was approaching her as an enemy or a friend. Chelsea took her finger from around the gun she had concealed in her hoodie as she looked up into Ant's smiling face. She had to admit he had swagger to be from down South.

"I'm sorry," she apologized. "You can never be too careful around here these days," she admitted.

"I know exactly what you mean," he agreed, making them both burst out into laughter. "My name is Anthony," he introduced himself, stepping out of the Range Rover.

"Chelsea." She blushed, placing her hand in his. To her surprise, Ant placed the back of her hand to his full lips. Chelsea tensed up when a chill went through her body.

"So where are you from down South?" she asked, catching Ant by surprise.

"Who said I was from down South?" he questioned suspiciously.

"Calm down, playboy. I can hear it in the way you pronounce your words," she answered.

"Man, I'm tripping," he said to himself and then

relaxed. "I'm from North Carolina," he answered without revealing his exact whereabouts. They made small talk for the better part of the hour, right in front of Jim's. The only thing that broke their conversation was the buzzing of Ant's cell phone. "Well, I got a few moves to make, shorty." Ant went into his pocket and pulled out a business card and then handed it to her. "Come check me out when you get the time." Chelsea looked at the card as Ant climbed back into his truck. She watched him back up and pull out into traffic, before making her way back to her vehicle. "The Queen's Palace." She smiled and then thumped the card in her hand. After reciting the number on the back of the card, she slid it into her handbag, started her car, and then began to put her plan into motion. She was looking for a quick come-up on the lick of a lifetime. "Only time will tell," she said to herself. She pulled away from the curb and headed back home to Newark.

3

It took a few days of searching through his files, but Detective Bass finally stumbled on the folder he was looking for. After clapping his hands together, Detective Bass picked up the phone on his desk and punched in three numbers. "Come to my office ASAP," he ordered. He then hung up in the caller's ear before they got the chance to respond. Two minutes later there was a knock at his door before it slowly crept open.

"What the hell are you smiling so hard for?" Green asked as he cautiously made his way across the room to where his partner sat behind his desk.

Detective Alvin Green had been with Trenton Police Department for five years, joining a year after Detective Bass. Being that Green was a little on the wild side and loved to take chances, Bass took him up under his wing and began to mold him. It paid off because it only took Green ten months of hard work and dedication for him to respectfully earn a nickname, "The Bloodhound," for his ability to sniff out things that took others months to find.

Once Green made himself comfortable in the chair that sat in front of Bass's desk, Bass flipped open the folder that sat in front of him and then turned it around and slid it to Green. Detective Green looked over the photos, confused, and then slid them back across the desk to his partner. "Okay, now you are investigating a dead man's case again?" Green asked. He shook his head like his partner had lost his mind. Bass and Green worked the King case a year straight, day and night, and were never able to get a good lead on him. Even when they got one of his workers to help them with the case, King seemed to slip away. Right when they were closing in on him, King up and got himself murdered, and out of all nights, on the night they were supposed to bring him down.

"Not him, you ass. The woman in the picture with him." Bass turned the folder back around and pointed to the beautiful woman with neatly twisted locks cascading over her breasts. Green took a closer look and had to admit the woman in the picture was definitely a sight to see. By the look on Green's face, Bass decided to help his partner out with where he was trying to go with things. "I was following up on a lead of one of my informants when I spotted her and another guy coming out of Dee-Dee's Bar and Lounge down on Brunswick Avenue."

"Oh boy. Here we go with one of your leads from your so-called informants again," Green huffed and then shook his head. Most of Bass's leads from his informants came up blank nine times out of ten, and he wondered if this was just another one of those leads.

"Man! Just shut up and listen!"

Green leaned back in the chair and let Bass continue with his story. "Anyway. I watched the guy escort the lady into the back of a new Bentley truck and then hop in the front seat. I waited for them to get a few blocks away before I pulled them over." Now Bass had Green's attention.

"So, what did you find?"

"Nothing."

"Nothing?" Green frowned his face up. Green knew if he had stopped the vehicle, he would have found at least some type of violation of something. "Man, you tripping!" Green shouted. He then stood to his feet ready to make his exit, until Bass stopped him.

"Green. They were driving a brand-new Bentley truck in the middle of the hood; a well-known drug and crime area and no one even bothered to try and steal it or vandalize it. Don't you find that kind of strange?" Bass pointed out. Green hated to admit it, but Bass was right, and things all started to make sense, at least a little sense for the moment. Green took his seat once again and decided to entertain what his partner was getting down to.

"Let me guess this since I know you so well. I bet you my last dollar you think this pretty young lady here"— Green pointed at the picture of Tawana—"took over King's business when he died?"

"Bingo." Bass snapped his finger then reclined his seat.

"You're crazier than I thought." Green laughed and jumped to his feet. "Man, I'm outta here." Green headed to the door.

"Ay, Green," Bass called out before his partner walked out of his office. Bass knew he wouldn't be able to crack the case without him and knew he had to find a way to get him onboard. Green turned around holding his stomach trying to control his laughter. "You trying to go to the strip club tonight?" Green's laughter ceased and his face became serious.

"And you knoooooow it!" Green grinned, and that's when Bass knew solving the case wouldn't be as hard as he thought it would be with his partner by his side.

4

Crystal rode down Route 1 heading south, back to Trenton from Newark. She decided to take the long way instead of hopping on the turnpike, since she was running a little ahead of schedule and needed to burn some time. "Quaker Bridge Mall," she read the big sign to her left and then took the next exit. She had visited the mall a few days earlier and had seen the cutest pair of white-and-blue Jordans for Junior that she just had to get him.

Once she found a good parking space up close to the entrance, Crystal hopped out of her mint-green Jag. She reached over her shoulder and hit the alarm button as she made her way through the parking lot. CHIRP-CHIRP Even though Crystal had a selection of luxury vehicles, she preferred to drive her Jag. Not because it was low-key, but because it once belonged to her late boyfriend, Menace, and she believed every time she drove it to do her dirt, he was looking over her.

Crystal stood inside the Foot Locker with her I-Phone

glued to her ear waiting for the sales clerk to come assist her. "Look boy, I don't got time to come pick you up before I go over to The Queen's Palace," she assured Ant after sucking her teeth. Before she could continue, the sales clerk approached her and smiled. Crystal returned her smile and held up five fingers, indicating the size shoe she needed.

"I'll be right back, ma'am." Crystal let out a deep breath and rolled her eyes as she listened to Ant give her a thousand and one reasons why he needed her to come pick him up instead of driving his own car.

"Okay, boy, dag!" Crystal gave in. She looked up and saw the sales clerk flagging her over to the counter to complete her purchase. After smiling a victorious grin, Ant assured Crystal he would be ready by eleven o'clock sharp, then ended the call. She knew if she wanted to make it to the club on time, she needed to be up and out of the mall in the next five minutes.

"That'll be $74.93, please." Crystal reached into her handbag to grab her credit card to pay for the purchase. As soon as her hand touched her black card, she heard a silky voice speak from behind her.

"Please. Allow me."

Crystal turned around slowly, ready to put the man in his place.

"I—," she began, but her words got caught in her throat when her eyes landed on the figure in front of her. Instead of waiting for her reply, he reached into of his linen jacket and retrieved his wallet. Crystal looked at the red stitching on the inside of his jacket and then down at his feet. She had a real shoe fetish, and the matching Gucci red bottoms set his outfit off to a *T*. She had to admit he was very suave, but she really was not into dating anyone outside of her race. Crystal watched the cashier take his card, swipe it, and then hand it back to him along with the receipt.

"Thank you, Mr. Sanchez." The sales clerk smiled once he signed his John Hancock on the dotted line.

"The pleasure was all mine, Amanda." Sanchez smiled and then directed his attention back to Crystal.

"Well, Mr. Sanchez," Crystal mocked the sales clerk. "It was nice meeting you, but I have to get going." Crystal grabbed her bag from the counter and then slung it over her shoulder.

"Please, call me Jay." Sanchez smiled.

"Okay, Jay."

"And you are?"

Crystal blushed and told him her name.

"What a beautiful name for a precious jewel like yourself."

"Thank you," she found herself saying. Any other time someone would've tried to hit her with the corny line, she would have put him in his place, but Jay was different. She looked at her watch and then cursed. Right when she was about to tell him she had to go for the second time, he handed her his card. To his surprise, she handed him her business card as well. After exchanging numbers, Crystal hurried out of the Foot Locker to her car. When she pulled off, she looked back in her rearview mirror and spotted Jay being escorted into the back of a black stretched Hummer. "Who is this man?" she thought to herself as she crossed over Route 1. She rounded the ben and then merged onto the busy interstate.

Even though Crystal didn't have the slightest idea who the mystery man was, she had a good idea of who could help her find out. After giving B.B. all of the information she had on her new friend, Crystal ended the call and headed home to get ready for the night that lay ahead of her.

~ ~ ~

After walking Junior over to the west wing of the mansion, Tawana headed back to the east wing to her master bedroom to get herself ready to go to The Queen's Palace. Since she had to walk past Crystal's room on the way, she decided to stick her head in and let her know what she had found out about Jay. "He owns a string of restaurants from New York all the way down to Florida," Tawana informed. "He also has a few used car lots and salvage yards as well. Other than that, he is squeaky clean." After applying lip liner to her glossy lips, Crystal pressed them together. It was hard for her to believe that was all Jay was into. It was just something about him that made her think differently. "What are you over there smiling about?" Tawana asked looking over Crystal's shoulder into the mirror at her reflection. Crystal looked into the mirror and noticed the glow on her face as well.

"Girl, ain't nobody smiling." Crystal stood up and looked away. She made her way over to the walk-in closet to find the perfect pair of stilettos to go with her La Perla pants set. When Crystal stepped out of her closet, she decided to ask about Tawana and Tamar to change the subject. She knew how much Tamar was feeling her, and even though Tawana never admitted it, Crystal knew her sister was feeling him too. "I know this bitch didn't," Crystal cursed when she turned around and noticed Tawana was no longer standing in her room. "I hate when she do that shit!" Crystal walked over to the nightstand beside her bed and grabbed her handbag and keys and was on her way. She knew if she wanted to make it to the strip club on time, she had to leave now because Ant was worse than a female when it came to getting dressed.

~ ~ ~

"What took you so damn long?" Crystal fumed when Ant finally got into the car. "I swear you are worse than a female when it comes to getting dressed." Ant placed the book bag full of money on the floorboard, between his legs, and then looked over at her.

"I look good, don't I?" Ant smiled and then popped his collar. Crystal had to admit Ant was looking damn good in his Gucci slacks and button-up, but she would never let him know that.

"You clean up alright." Even though it wasn't much of a compliment, Ant took it in stride since it was coming from Crystal. Crystal hit the Start button and the GS 350 Lex came to life.

When they pulled to the front of The Queen's Palace, it was like a car and fashion show outside. Everybody that was anybody was there that night, from professional ball players to politicians. Even a few celebrities came out to play. Ant checked his attire one last time before hopping out like a superstar himself. To Crystal's surprise, Ant got quite a few stares. What really surprised her was when he came around to the driver's side and opened her door for her to step out. Crystal put her hand in his, and it was as if every eye in line watched her long, silky-smooth legs step out of the car. They walked arm in arm down the red carpet that lined the sidewalk to the front entrance of the building. Once the bouncers saw the couple, they didn't even bother to search the book bag Ant had draped over his shoulder.

The first thing they saw when they walked into the building was big kitties and even bigger asses bouncing and jiggling to Black Beetles. "I'ma have me some fun tonight," Ant claimed, rubbing his hands together. He stopped a topless stripper and began fondling her goods.

"Boy, give me that damn book bag," Crystal snapped. She didn't even give Ant time to slide it off of his shoulder. Ant smiled after Crystal snatched the book bag. He knew Crystal was uptight about him feeling up the stripper in front of her, but that was part of his plan. By the way she reacted, he knew he was wearing her down and would have her by his side in no time. He watched her head to the stairs on the other side of the club. Once Bo let her through, he really went in on the stripper.

Tawana looked up from her laptop on her desk when Crystal stormed into her office. "You okay?" she asked as Crystal made her way over to the two-way mirror on the wall that overlooked the lower level of the crowded strip club below. After getting no response, Tawana stood to her feet and joined her sister to see what had her attention. "I knew it," she shouted accusingly. She felt Crystal had a thing for Ant when she first introduced them, but Crystal would always downplay or deny it. Now the proof was in the pudding.

"Bitch please." Crystal sucked her teeth and rolled her eyes and then walked over behind Tawana's desk. She placed the book bag on the desk before taking a seat in Tawana's chair. Tawana watched Ant stroll over to the VIP section of the club with a stripper on his arm before she turned around.

"So how are things going with the spots?" Tawana asked as she made her way back over to her desk. She took a seat on the edge of her desk, looked inside the book bag, and then closed it back up.

"Things couldn't be better," she admitted with a smile on her face. Money was the only thing that could make her feel better and get her mind off of Ant at the time. Crystal looked at her watch before continuing. "Oh yeah, our clientele from Newport News, Virginia, should be here anytime now. They gonna drop the money off, and once we hit them off tomorrow, they will be back on the highway heading back to 'Bad News.'" That was like music to Tawana's ears because once they hit the VA crew off, they would be ready to re-up with Tamar again. Crystal noticed her sister staring off into space with a huge smile on her face. "What's on your mind?" Crystal questioned.

"Nothing," Tawana answered.

"Ummm-hmmm," Crystal responded with her mouth twisted to the side.

The truth was, ever since Tawana, Crystal, Ant, and Junior returned to New Jersey, her life was going just the way she had planned it, and she couldn't have been happier. Tawana grabbed the book bag off her desk and walked over to the wall and removed the picture of her and King. Behind it sat the door to the safe and beside it was the digital combination pad.

"Don't give me that 'nothing' bullshit," Crystal cursed. She walked back over to the two-way mirror to look over the establishment. She was so lost in seeing what Ant was doing, she never heard Tawana speaking to her until she was up in her ear. "Huh, what you say?"

Tawana shook her head from side to side. "I said," she began with a roll of her eyes, "I'm thinking about retiring."

"You what?" Crystal asked, thinking she heard her sister wrong. She had a disbelieving look on her face until Tawana confirmed herself. Crystal was more confused than ever. Business was booming. As a matter of fact, it had been doing better than it ever had been doing before, even when King was running it.

"Why?"

Tawana walked away and took a seat behind her desk. After pressing a few buttons on her laptop, she turned it around to Crystal.

"This is why." Crystal looked at the screen, and a picture of Tawana and Junior was on display. It was the picture she took of them the week before when they went to Six Flags. After realizing what Tawana was insinuating, a warm and loving smile appeared on Crystal's face. She knew what Tawana was silently asking her, and she felt it was only right to give it to her. "You know you have my blessings, bitch!" Crystal squeezed out. Then she ran over to her sister and gave her a big hug.

"You know I couldn't have done none of this without you, right?" Tawana questioned seriously. Even though Crystal knew Tawana was right, she twisted her mouth to the side and waved her off like it was nothing.

"Anywayyyyy. So, when you gonna get you a man?"

Crystal quickly asked, changing the subject. Tawana knew the question would soon surface, but to be honest, she didn't even have an answer to it. Her last relationship had ended badly. As a matter of fact, the one before that ended the same exact way.

She reflected back to her last boyfriend, King. He was the only father figure Junior ever knew in his life. That was, until his biological father, Speedy, came and took him away from her. It was by the grace of God she got Junior back safely. That was the day Tawana vowed to protect him by any means necessary. Crystal went on pressing Tawana until Tawana stopped her.

"Okay. Okay. I tell you what. I'll go out with Tamar, IF you go out with this guy Jay you made me investigate," Tawana negotiated. The only reason she entertained the idea was because she knew Crystal hadn't thought about a man seriously since Menace was killed. Also because she knew her sister was not the type of woman to date outside of her race. At least that's what she thought.

"BET!" Crystal shouted sealing the deal. If it wasn't for the fact that Tawana was already sitting down, she would have hit the floor. Crystal turned and walked back over to the two-way mirror. That gave Tawana a little hope that Crystal would back out of their deal. Now she had to figure out a way to get Ant to step up his game and make a move before it was too late. "So, when are you going to holla at Tamar and see what's up?"

"I guess when I see him." Tawana looked down at her laptop at the picture on the screen once again. "What, bitch?" Tawana asked, noticing Crystal staring over at her with a huge smile on her face.

"Guess who just walked up in the place?" Crystal asked. She then looked down at the club entrance. Tawana got up out of her seat, almost knocking it over, and stood beside her sister. "Go on down there!" Crystal urged excitedly, grabbing Tawana by the arm and ushering her to the door. Once she was on her way down the stairs, Crystal made her way back to the two-way mirror to get a front-row seat. As she waited for Tawana to come into view, her sight landed on Ant. Immediately, Crystal's blood started to boil at what she saw in front of her.

~ ~ ~

It was as if everything moved in slow motion for

Tawana as she made her way downstairs. "Here goes nothing," she said, trying to pump herself up to go over to Tamar. It wasn't that she was shy, she just never pursued a man. All her life, men flocked to her. This was something new to her. Tawana walked up behind Tamar and stood on her tiptoes. "I see you took the time out of your busy schedule to stop by The Queen's Palace," Tawana seductively whispered in his ear, catching him and his two bodyguards by surprise. Tamar turned around and looked Tawana up and down before responding.

"And what a beautiful queen you are," he complimented before taking her hand in his and kissing the back of it. Tawana found herself blushing from his touch.

"Allow me to give you a tour of the place," she offered. Tamar nodded to his bodyguards, and they walked over to a nearby booth to watch the brown-skinned baby doll on stage do her thing. Tamar followed Tawana down a slim hallway with several doors on each side, until they reached the one at the very end with the words Elite Members Only above the door.

"Wow. I'm impressed," Tamar admitted. Not only

was the huge area decorated in his favorite colors, black and gold, but he could also smell the expensive Italian leather on the sectionals placed all around the room.

"Come," Tawana tugged at the tie Tamar had hanging from his neck, pulling him into one of the rooms off to the side and closing the door behind them. Inside were more sectionals, a bar, and their own personal strippers that danced on the stage that sat in the middle of the room. As soon as they took their seats on the sectional, they were greeted by a topless waitress with a bottle of Dom P in a chilled bucket of ice. "Thank you, Amanda." Amanda bowed gracefully and then turned to head back to her spot behind the bar, until Tamar stopped her.

"Thank you." She nodded after taking the hundred-dollar bill from his hand. Tamar watched her heart-shaped ass jiggle across the room.

"Well, Mr. Tamar, what brings you to my neck of the woods?" Tawana asked, snapping him away from his thoughts of bending the waitress over and beating her back out.

"I remembered you giving me an invitation to stop by when I got the time, so, I had the time," he answered as he slid out of his suit jacket and adjusted his gold cufflinks. Tamar crossed one leg over the other and then placed both arms wide and rested them on the back of the booth's seats. Tawana hated to admit it, but she was turned on by Tamar's arrogant swagger.

"No, tell me why you are really here," Tawana said as she placed a hand on his thigh. Caught off guard by Tawana's aggressiveness, Tamar sat straight up and looked into her eyes. He didn't know what kind of game Tawana was playing, since every time he tried to make advances on her, she always shot him down.

"You know why I'm here," he answered boldly. Tawana moved her hand up Tamar's thigh slowly as she leaned forward into his personal space until their lips collided. Tamar closed his eyes when Tawana brushed his crotch and began to unzip his slacks. It wasn't until he felt a set of warm and wet lips wrap around his erection he opened his eyes. Tawana removed her lips from his and smiled at the confused look on Tamar's face. When he looked down, the two strippers that were dancing onstage when they first came in were now taking turns sucking his joystick like a lollipop. Before he got the chance to say a word, Crystal rushed into the room.

"Tawana!" she yelled out heatedly. "Oh, I'm sorry," she apologized after barging in and literally catching Tamar with his pants down.

"Please excuse me." Tawana slid off of the sectional as Crystal turned and walked out the door. Before Tawana walked out, she turned and looked back at Tamar. "Enjoy yourself." Tamar didn't know how to respond, so he did the first thing that came to mind. Tawana shook her head and saluted him back before stepping into the hall and closing the door behind herself.

As soon as the door closed, Crystal began with her tantrum. "Girl, I got to get out of here before I fuck around and punch Ant in his damn face. Do you know he out there with a bitch's head buried in his damn lap. He is so disrespectful!" Crystal went on for another minute or two until she heard her sister snicker. "What the hell are you laughing at, Tawana?"

"Hold up, Crystal. I don't mean to laugh, but aren't you the one that said Ant is not your type and you don't like nor want him?" Crystal stood there silently with her arms folded over her chest as Tawana stared at her,

56

waiting for some kind of response.

"I'll see you in the morning," Crystal said, defeated. She headed out of the elite VIP entrance. Tawana called after her sister, but she kept walking. Tawana stood there until the door closed behind Crystal.

~ ~ ~

As soon as Crystal stepped out from the elite VIP section of the club, she felt a strong hand grip her shoulder. After snatching away, she turned to address the person who had disrespected her in the worst way. Her facial expression softened when she laid eyes on Chee-Chee.

Chee-Chee was Crystal's client out of Newport News, Virginia. She met the six-foot-tall, clean-cut, action-figure-looking hustler one afternoon while she was vacationing at Virginia Beach a few years back. After a long dinner and a night full of lustful sex, they found out they had a lot in common, with the drug game being at the top of their list. That's what led him to Trenton that night.

"Whoa, calm down. It's just me." Chee-Chee smiled then took a step back.

"Yo ass was about to get cut," Crystal warned. She then licked her tongue out, revealing a brand-new razor lying on top of it.

"You got that," Chee replied, remembering the way Crystal handled one of his side chicks that got out of line one day when he brought her along to handle business when Crystal came to Newport News on business.

"Boy, I ain't messing with you," Crystal said, waving him off after reading his mind. Chee-Chee laughed after he followed Crystal across the crowded room to the bar. He watched her ass bounce every which-a-way until they reached their destination. Once she ordered them both a bottle of champagne, Crystal got down to business. "The same as usual?" she asked, looking down at the briefcase he set on the floor between them.

"Double that," he responded without blinking.

"Damn! Shit jumping like that?" she questioned, surprised.

"And it's gonna stay like that as long as you keep the good shit you got," he assured her as the bartender sat the bottles on the bar top. Crystal nodded in approval.

"I'll call you around noon with your package," she

informed him. She then grabbed her bottle by the neck.

"To new beginnings," Chee-Chee toasted.

"To new beginnings," Crystal agreed. They both popped their corks at the same time in celebration. After downing half of the bottle in one gulp, Chee-Chee said his good-byes.

"You leaving so soon?" Crystal asked. She secretly wanted to accompany him at his hotel room later on that night.

"I wish I could stay," he told her after seeing the disappointment in her eyes. "I got 'her' with me." Even though Crystal was in her feelings, she had to respect "her," being that she knew he was already in a committed relationship when they hooked up from time to time. "I got you when you come to my part of town," he promised, then snaked his tongue out at her. The thought of the many things he did to her with his tongue gave Crystal the shivers.

"I'ma hold you to that too." Chee-Chee held his bottle to his lips once again, and when he put it back down, it was empty.

"You do that." Chee-Chee winked his eye and then

turned and walked away leaving Crystal with wet panties and thoughts of her next trip to VA. After getting herself together, Crystal headed upstairs to Tawana's office to put the money away with the rest of the cash in the wall safe.

When she was done, she walked over to the two-way wall mirror and looked down at the crowd. To her surprise, Ant was no longer in his VIP booth. In a way, Crystal was glad because she really didn't want to see him right now because there was no telling what she might do. Once she locked up, Crystal packed up and headed home.

~ ~ ~

Ant sat in the VIP booth with a stripper's face buried in his lap. "Shit!" he cursed as her teeth accidentally scraped over his shaft. "Get the fuck up!" He helped assist her by snatching her head up by her weave.

"Ouch! I'm sorry, Ant," she apologized before he slung her forcefully out of his booth. Even though he didn't get his rocks off, he still threw a couple hundred at her. After picking her earnings up off the floor, the stripper scurried away, embarrassed. Ant placed his throbbing member back in his pants before zipping them back up and then headed for the door. He had a long day ahead of him and decided to call it a night. "It can't be," he thought to himself when he spotted a familiar frame standing at the bar. "Put her tab on my bill," Ant told the barmaid when he made his way over to the bar. Chelsea looked over at Ant with a smile on her face.

"I see you like to buy me things," she joked, teasingly.

"Nothing comes free," he replied, looking her up and down. Ant had to admit she was a far cry from the first time they had met. Her loose-fitting jogging suit was replaced by a pair of skintight 7 jeans, a matching T-shirt, and a pair of red-bottom heels.

Chelsea smiled knowingly as the barmaid returned with her bottle. "I'll drink to that," she agreed. She then popped the top of her champagne. Moet fizzed from the top and ran onto the bar top. Chelsea filled her flute up to the top and made a toast. "To new friends." Ant lifted the entire bottle in the air and toasted.

"To new friends," Ant said and then downed half of the bottle. When he placed it down on the counter, he looked over at Chelsea again. "You driving?"

Chelsea smiled and held up the key fob to her Beamer.

"Yep," she answered before finishing off her flute.

"Come on," he demanded as he took her key fob out of her hand and headed for the exit. Chelsea took one last sip of her flute before marching out of the strip club behind him.

"I see you remember what kind of car I drive," she said when she hopped in the passenger seat of her BMW. Instead of responding, Ant put the car in drive and then headed out of the parking lot. "May I ask where you are taking me?" Still no response. Getting nowhere with her questions. Chelsea sat back, put on her seatbelt, and enjoyed the ride.

Thirty minutes later, they were cruising through the streets of Ewing, New Jersey. After punching in the code at the front entrance, the gates slid apart, and Ant drove into the gated condominiums. "This is nice," Chelsea admitted as Ant pulled up to a row of vehicles under a shelter. After finding a space between the Range Rover he drove the day she met him and a black-on-black SRT Challenger, Ant killed the engine.

Chelsea followed Ant into his home, up a flight of stairs, and to his bedroom. She was quite amazed at his bachelor's pad. She turned to face him to compliment him on his taste, but got caught off guard when Ant wrapped his arms around her waist and placed his tongue in her mouth. "Mmmm," she moaned as he massaged her ass gently. Once she was lifted off of her feet, Ant carried her across the room to his king-size bed and laid her down. They clawed at each other's clothes until they were heated and naked.

"Turn over," Ant demanded with his shaft in his hands. Chelsea did as she was told and tooted her ass up in the air giving him complete control.

To Chelsea's surprise, Ant knew how to work what he had been blessed with. "Beat this pussy, Anthony!" she ordered, meeting him thrust for thrust. Ant's stamina was a little more than Chelsea had estimated, so she ended up flipping the script. "Let me ride this big dick," she said, boosting his already big ego. Ant pulled out of her wetness and lay in the center of the bed.

"Damn, girl," Ant cursed as Chelsea rocked and bucked on his rod. Three minutes later, Ant's body tensed up and she had him calling out her name with his toes curling up like the Wicked Witch of the East. After he filled her up with his seeds, they lay in each other's arms.

~ ~ ~

For the next couple of days, Ant and Chelsea couldn't get enough of each other, and the following week, she began moving her things into his place. Every chance they got, they sexed each other's brains out. Everything was going according to plan for Chelsea. The only bad thing was she was starting to catch feelings for Ant, and she hoped she could go through with things.

Only time would tell, but until then, she was going to enjoy every minute of him. All the way to the end, she promised herself, running her fingers through his hair as he lapped up her sweet juices with her tongue. "Right there," she coached when he hit her G-spot. Shortly after, Ant was up on his feet and Chelsea was returning the favor.

5

Hadji had been cooped up in his rest haven for the past few weeks as he recovered from his gunshot wound. He wasn't quite 100 percent, but he was a far cry from when he first came home. The same could not be said for his broken heart. His mind could not grasp the fact that the love of his life, his wife, his soul mate, had shot and tried to kill him. The look in her eyes when he heard the gunshot ring out through the air, right before it felt like he got hit in his chest with a sledgehammer, played over and over in his mind. On top of that, Sherry refused to let him come see her. Even though Hadji respected her wishes, Jamontae, Diontae, and even Mya, who was upset with him, kept him updated on her current condition, which was getting better. Sherry's memory had been lost at first , but was now slowly coming back to her. What confused him the most was Mya telling him Sherry was telling her she didn't shoot Hadji. He hoped once her memory was fully back, she could give him a reason for her actions. Until then, he would wait patiently for her to come back around to the old her, the woman he fell in love with when he first saw her.

He remembered back to the first time he laid eyes on her at his cousin Erica's beauty salon.

"G.U. Kutts-N-Styles," Hadji read out loud as he looked up at the big blue letters that were displayed across the front window of the establishment. When he stepped out of his car, he noticed there was only one car outside besides Erica's candy-apple red Camaro. "She must be on her last client for the day," he thought to himself as he walked up and entered the shop. "Where do you want me to put these?" he asked as he held the supplies in the air.

"You can put them over beside the wash bowl," she answered. "How much do I owe you?" She continued to style her client's hair without once looking in his direction. Hadji thought long and hard before he answered.

"You can pay for dinner and we will be even." Erica agreed with a sigh of relief, knowing she was getting off the hook easily. Hadji took a seat at one of the styling chairs, picked up a GQ magazine, and began flipping through it. When he got halfway through the book, he felt his stomach starting to growl. He prayed he had not gotten one of his jump-offs pregnant again.

Thirty minutes later, Erica was handing her client a handheld mirror so she could look at the back of her hair in the large mirror behind her. "Hadji, how does Sherry's hair look?" He was not paying any attention to her client's hair. He was still trying to figure out where they were going to eat for dinner. He wanted to just say it looked good, just to hurry up with the process, but instead he put the magazine down just as Erica stood to the side to give him a clear view. Hadji felt like a deer stuck in headlights when he saw the beautiful woman upon him. He stared in awe as he took in everything about her. She showed off her pearly white teeth when she smiled and her evenly toned silky and flawless chocolate skin all complimented her oversized brown Fendi handbag. The way she stood showed she was very confident with herself and, not to mention, sexy.

"Beautiful," Hadji finally answered as he stood to his feet.

He remembered that day as if it was the day before. "I gotta get out of this house," he said, more to himself looking around at all the pictures hanging in the living room of him and Sherry. That had been his bedroom since he returned home. He was unable to sleep in their bedroom the first night, thinking that would get his mind off of Sherry. He chose the living room, which was proving not to be any better.

Hadji picked himself up off the couch and took his cell off of the charger and made his morning call. After Jamontae informed him Sherry would be released in a couple of days, he ended the call. He knew the day would eventually come, but he wasn't so sure he was quite ready. He knew he wanted her home and out of the hospital. He just didn't know if he was ready to face the music yet.

After looking at all of the missed calls from Slim, Fuzzy, and the rest of the crew, Hadji began to go through his voicemails to clear them out. He knew he would have a lot of voicemails, but he didn't think it would be totally full.

By the time Hadji finished listening to and deleting all of the old voicemails, he had watched an entire episode of *In Living Color*. Out of all the messages he had on his phone, Hadji only saved one: *"Hello stranger. This is Cee-Cee. Long time no hear from. It's fucked up I had to get your number from someone else instead of you giving it to me. I thought we were better than that. Anyway, when you get this message, hit a bitch back. I got some news*

I'm sure you will be interested in hearing." Cee-Cee repeated her number and Hadji stored it in his cell. He hadn't spoken to Cee-Cee since he and Sherry tied the knot. The last he heard, she had moved out of town.

Hadji stood to his feet and headed upstairs to his bedroom to gather his clothes, take a shower, and get himself together. He had a long day ahead of him and planned to get a few things done around the house before Sherry came home.

After dressing, Hadji made it downstairs and to the kitchen to make his exit to the jointed garage. His heart dropped when he first stepped into the garage, and then it hit him. Getting up with the twins would be the first thing on his to-do list for the day to get his NSX back. He had forgotten all about trading cars with them and that their car was still at Fuzzy's place since he was driving it when he got shot. That also meant he had to call Fuzzy, something he was not looking forward to at the time but had to be done. Walking past the spot where his Acura usually sat, Hadji took a few steps further to his Lexus Coupe.

All sorts of memories resurfaced when he sat in the driver's seat. The one that came to mind first was the one of him calling his cousin Sean, God bless the dead, and telling him he had found the woman of his dreams. No matter how hard Hadji tried to get her off his mind, things always seemed to find their way back to Sherry. Sean had laughed at Hadji, but six months later, he was the best man at their wedding. After adjusting the rearview mirror, Hadji pressed the button on the garage opener and watched the door lift up, and then he backed out. Before he even got off his block, he was dialing the twins' number. "Meet me at Club Drama in an hour." After a short conversation, he ended the call and called Fuzzy and told her the same thing. Before she got the chance to tell him what was on her mind, Hadji disconnected the call. Fuzzy knew why he wanted her to meet him at Drama, so once she was dressed, she snatched the keys to the twins' car and headed to her destination.

~ ~ ~

Fuzzy contemplated calling Slim to let him know she had finally spoken to Hadji and she was about to meet him at Club Drama, but knew if she did, he would be on the way before they even hung up the phone. She knew if he wanted Slim there, he would have called Slim himself.

When Fuzzy pulled up to the club, the first thing she spotted was Hadji's canary-yellow Acura NSX parked in front of the entrance. She looked around for another vehicle, but there was none in the lot. After parking, Fuzzy stepped out of the car and was greeted by the twin she knew as Malek. She knew it was him because he was the laidback. easy-going twin. The only one she actually had a conversation with the last time she saw them. The other twin, Maleki, was more to himself and only acknowledged Fuzzy with head nods. She made sure to keep a close eye on him. She was taught long ago to always watch silent people because they are the most dangerous. "Follow me." She smiled and led the way to the club entrance. "Hadji should be here any time now," she spoke over her shoulder as they walked inside of Drama.

"Have y'all heard anything about who was behind the attempt on Hadji and his wife's life?" Malek questioned as he and Maleki took a seat on the stool at the bar. Fuzzy was just about to respond, until she got sidetracked by the sound of her phone. She held up a finger and then answered it.

"Okay," she replied short, then headed to the back. Maleki reached in his waistline and put his hand on the butt of his pistol that was sticking out. He relaxed when Fuzzy re-entered the room with Hadji right behind her.

"How you feeling, bruh?" Malek asked as he stood to

71

his feet to show his friend some love.

"Ahhh," Hadji whined when Malek bumped chests with him.

"My bad, homie," he apologized and took a step back. By the look in Hadji's eyes, Malek could tell he was not at his best just yet. When Hadji looked over at Maleki, he saluted and Maleki did the same. Fuzzy made her way behind the bar and fixed everyone a much-needed drink.

"I'm good," Maleki rejected the drink and got down to business. "What happened with that thing the last time we saw y'all?" he asked, looking at Hadji for an answer. He saw on the news Lil Man and his baby mama had been killed in a warehouse fire. After giving the twins the short version of what went down at the warehouse, he went on and told what he remembered about getting shot at Fuzzy's place. It was still a blur to him, but he managed to remember bits and pieces of the day.

"Well, you know we got your back when you find out who's behind it, don't you?" Malek said, letting him know he was down for the cause.

"Yeah. You know we *'real'* family," Maleki added, looking in Fuzzy's direction. They locked eyes menacingly, neither one wanting to be the first to drop eye contact.

"Fuzzy," Hadji called out to her for the second time. She was so caught up in the stare down, she hadn't heard him until then. "Let me holla at them in private." Even though he was asking politely, she knew it was an order. Fuzzy cleared their glasses off the top of the bar and then headed to the back to put them away for the dishwasher that would be coming in later on that night when the club opened. When she was out of sight, Maleki spoke his mind.

"Man, I'd watch that bitch if I was you, Hadji," he warned. Before Hadji got the chance to reply, Fuzzy emerged from the back and walked up to Maleki. Hadji knew nothing good could come out of the stand-off, so he decided to intervene.

"Everything's good, Hadji," Fuzzy spoke, making Hadji pause in his step. Fuzzy reached in her pocket and pulled out the set of keys to the twins' car and then dropped them into Maleki's front pocket. "I'll be outside in the car waiting on you," she informed Hadji, never taking her eyes from Maleki. Before turning around to walk off, Fuzzy blew Maleki a kiss and then smiled. He smiled back. It was like a deadly game of cat and mouse was being played between the two, and Hadji knew it. Malek watched the sway in Fuzzy's hips until she disappeared out the front entrance.

"I'ma fuck around and end up bodying that bitch," Maleki promised as he rubbed his hands together. Hadji placed a hand on his friend's shoulder and gave it a slight squeeze.

"She good people, bruh," he assured the twin.

"Huh, if you say so." They chatted a little while longer before Hadji finally ended their meeting and walked them out the door. After they showed each other love, they all parted ways.

"Yo, what's his problem?" Fuzzy asked once Hadji pulled his door down and sat in his car. She watched the twins pull out of the parking lot as she waited for a response.

"He's like that with everyone. You just got to get to know him," Hadji answered as he reached up and adjusted his rearview mirror. Once it was to his liking, he hit a button on his door and the seat adjusted itself to its normal position. When the twins' car was out of sight, Fuzzy noticed Hadji's Lexus roll up beside them. She wondered who was driving it, but chose not to question him about it. Due to the 5 percent limo tint, it was impossible for her to see inside. When Hadji put the car in drive, Fuzzy leaned her seat all the way back and closed her eyes. A lot ran through her mind. All she wanted to do now was go home, get in her bed, and get some rest.

The ride back to Fuzzy's place was awkward. When she tried to strike up small conversations with Hadji, his answers were short. She was thankful when he finally pulled into the circular driveway in front of the mansion. Before she could grab the door handle to lift the door into the air, Hadji stopped her. "It's not you. I just got a lot on my mind right now. I'll call you later." Fuzzy relaxed and smiled. She had something to tell him but couldn't find the words. When she did, the passenger side door lifted up and Jamontae was there to assist her out of the car.

"That's who was in his Lexus," she concluded. She turned around to speak, but Hadji cut her off.

"We'll talk about it later," he assured her, looking straight ahead. He had a feeling she was going to answer about what happened with them the night before he got shot, when he stayed the night. He desperately wanted to know, but he was more afraid of her answer than anything else. He was snapped from his thoughts by the sound of a light tap on his driver's-side window. Once he hit the button and the window came down, he stuck his hand out the window and placed a set of keys in Diontae's hand

and ordered him to get in Sherry's car and follow him and Jamontae to his place. Jamontae came back down the steps from walking Fuzzy to the door and lowered Hadji's passenger door. Once they were both in their assigned cars, Hadji put his car in drive. Before he pulled off of the estate, he looked up at Fuzzy's bedroom window. No matter how much he tried to deny it, she was beautiful and even more deadly. Hadji drove off of the estate with Jamontae and Diontae in tow. He had played the game and had gotten burnt, badly. Fuzzy stood at her window with her head propped up against the window pane. She knew her feelings for Hadji ran deep and if she ever wanted to be with him, she would have to take her secret to the grave with her, and that, she was willing to do.

After Jamontae and Diontae dropped Sherry and Hadji's car off at his place, Hadji dropped them off at the hospital to keep a close eye on Sherry. With the attempted murderer still at large, he couldn't take the chance at them trying to kill her again. He laughed to himself as he pulled off and looked in his rearview mirror at the brothers giving each other high fives as they entered the hospital's entrance. He had somehow let them talk him into going out with them to Club Drama that weekend. He just hoped he could avoid Fuzzy that night.

~ ~ ~

Hadji found himself ducked off in a booth in the far corner of VIP. It was the same booth Lil Man and Tank occupied when they ran the establishment. It gave Hadji a clear view of everyone who came and went from VIP. He felt like a sitting duck not knowing who was out to take his life. Hadji wasn't for sure, but he had a feeling B.B. and Ant were somehow involved in the attempt on his life; if not directly, indirectly. B.B. had to be pulling the strings because no one else in the town had the money nor the balls to go up against Hadji and the family/crew. For some strange reason, he had a feeling he knew Tawana, especially by the name Black Beauty. He just couldn't put the pieces of the puzzle together. His thoughts were interrupted when a barmaid approached his booth with a bottle of Moet in her hands. "You must be mistaken, because I didn't order anything to drink," he stopped her before she could place the bucket on the table. Embarrassed, the barmaid looked over at the bar and then back at Hadji.

"It's on the house." She smiled and then tilted her head in the direction of the bar. Hadji followed her head nod and found Fuzzy behind the bar looking over at him. Hadji looked back at the barmaid and let her place the bucket in the center of the table.

"Thank you, Mia." Hadji smiled apologetically and then reached into his pocket to tip her.

"No need. That's already been taken care of." Hadji watched Mia make her way back behind the bar to take care of the other patrons in VIP. That's when he noticed Fuzzy making her way over to him. Before she made it to his booth, Jamontae and Diontae appeared out of nowhere. Hadji breathed a sigh of relief when he saw Fuzzy redirect herself to the other side of the club.

"We thought you were going to be a no-show," Jamontae admitted as he removed the bottle of champagne from the bucket of ice and began pouring himself a drink.

"Nah, I try to keep my word, youngster," Hadji admitted. feeling a little insulted. There was a brief moment of silence.

"Speak for yourself," Diontae spoke up as he poured himself a glass. The trio sat back in the booth sipping on champagne, watching the party-goers do their thing on the dance floor. Hadji had to admit coming out took his mind off Sherry, if only for a few hours. Jamontae and Diontae noticed the extra attention they were receiving by being in the presence of their general.

"Excuse me, gentleman, but I have to go to the restroom," Hadji announced as he stood to his feet. "Alone," he made it clear when they stood to their feet. Jamontae and Diontae kept a close eye on Hadji as he entered the restroom. "Damn," he cursed as he relieved himself inside one of the stalls. After hearing the bathroom door open and then close, Hadji got a funny feeling in his gut. Usually his gut was never wrong, and hearing it lock a second later let him know it was right. "Who's there?" he questioned as he pulled his gun out and rounded one in the chamber.

"It's me," he heard a familiar voice answer. Hadji opened the stall door and took a step out.

"What are you doing in here, Fuzzy?" Hadji asked, looking around as if he was in the wrong restroom.

"Well, this is my club," she joked to lighten up the mood. Hadji didn't laugh, so she became serious. "Hadji, you can't keep avoiding me. I've called and even texted you, which is something I don't like doing." Fuzzy looked into his eyes trying to find the right words to say, but only two seemed to find their way out. "I'm sorry." She meant it in more ways than one. They stared into each other's eyes until their lips touched. Hadji hated to admit it, but Fuzzy's lips felt good; damn good. "Not here," Fuzzy pleaded as Hadji reached down and ran his hand up her bare thigh. He removed his hand and took a step back. After catching her breath, Fuzzy adjusted her dress. "I'll see you after I close up," she told him, and then headed for the door. She didn't bother to wait for him to respond because by the look of the bulge in his pants, he wanted her as bad as she wanted him.

When Hadji walked out of the bathroom, Jamontae and Diontae were there waiting on him. Instead of going back to their booth, Hadji decided to call it a night. "I'll hit y'all up in the morning to run a few things down to y'all," he told them before giving them some love. To his surprise, when Hadji walked away, they were right behind him. He looked at them as if to say, "Where y'all going," but after looking over at the bar at Fuzzy, he knew they were only following orders.

After Jamontae and Diontae made sure Hadji made it home safely, they headed back to the club to see if they could get lucky and take a few chicks back to their place for the night.

Once Hadji went up to his bedroom, he took off all of his clothes and took a shower. When he finished, he lay across the bed naked and drifted off to sleep.

Hadji was awakened by the sound of the ADT alarm

system he had installed. He quickly jumped out of bed and grabbed his gun. Naked, he scaled the wall until he made it to the stairs. When he looked down the stairs, he could plainly see the intruder. "What's the gun for? I told you I would see you when I closed the club." Fuzzy opened her robe, revealing her nude body.

"Damn! I'm slipping," Hadji said to himself, remembering he forgot to lock the front door before he set the alarm.

"And what are you going to do with that big gun?" Fuzzy questioned seductively as she floated up the stairs. Hadji looked from the gun in his hand back to Fuzzy, who somehow was standing in front of him.

"Not that gun, this one." Before Hadji knew what was happening, Fuzzy aggressively grabbed his manhood and forcefully slammed his back against the wall, making him release the gun from his grip. As soon as it hit the floor, Fuzzy was all over him.

"Fuzzy, we can't do—" was all he got the chance to say before Fuzzy's tongue was in this mouth. She let out soft moans as Hadji's hand caressed her backside. Gripping his erection, Fuzzy wrapped one arm around his shoulders, and with cat-like speed, she hopped up and wrapped her legs around his waist. Hadji turned and placed Fuzzy's back up against the wall and looked at her perky breasts before licking his lips. He then realized he was fighting a battle he was surely losing. "Fuzzy, you got to go!" Fuzzy pouted and poked out her bottom lip like a child who just dropped her ice-cream cone.

"You mean to tell me you're gonna pass up all of this" she asked before removing her arm from around his neck and placing her hand inside of her wetness. When she brought it back up, she placed a finger on Hadji's lips. The smell of her juices made him feel like he was about to explode right then and there. Fuzzy began to rotate her hips, making his erection brush up against her opening. It was as if he was now hypnotized. That was, until Fuzzy used her toned legs around his waist to pull him in closer. Hadji felt himself slowly getting vacuumed into her love cave. "Oh, Hadji," she released after sucking in a mouth full of air, trying to adjust to his length. Hadji felt like he was in heaven. Fuzzy arched her back against the wall, giving Hadji access to all she had to offer. Hadji pounded Fuzzy to the sound of the alarm beeping throughout the house. "Oh, Hadji, I'm about to cum!" Fuzzy screamed out in pleasure. Seconds later, he could feel her release all over his rod. He felt himself about to reach his climax also, and right before he did, Fuzzy whispered in his ear,

"I love you, Hadji," making him lose his focus.

The sound of the constant buzzing of his alarm made him open his eyes. Hadji looked over at the alarm clock and hit the snooze button. "Damn, that was a fucked-up dream," he said to himself as he focused his eyes on the clock to look at the time. He looked around the room to make sure he was in his own place this time. He breathed a sigh of relief seeing he was. "Man, I gotta stop drinking," he whispered. He then grabbed the sides of his head to stop the room from spinning. When he sat up, he had to laugh at himself. On his inner thigh was a big, wet, sticky area. Stiff legged, Hadji slid out of bed and headed to the bathroom to take a much-needed shower.

After showering, Hadji took his cell off the charger to check his messages. He had two missed calls, one voicemail, and three text messages. The missed calls were Fuzzy and Slim, one of the texts was from Cee-Cee informing him to get at her as soon as possible, another was from Slim telling him to give him a call, and the last text read: *I guess you are sleep. I'll see you another time, Fuzzy!* Hadji quickly deleted the text and set his phone on the nightstand. Thinking of Cee-Cee, he made a mental note to give her a call later on in the day after he finished handling a few things that needed to be handled. Once

Hadji was dressed, he headed out the door. He had to put his ears to the streets to try to figure out who wanted him dead and who could have known his exact whereabouts. He figured it had to be someone in a high position to be able to get on the grounds of Fuzzy's estate, considering the top-notch surveillance she had around the fortress. "That's it." Hadji smiled. "Why didn't I think of that at first?" Hadji jumped in his NSX and sped off out of the cul-de-sac. He was going to get down to the bottom of it even if it killed him.

6

Detectives Bass and Green sat in an old utility van they used as an undercover stakeout vehicle. They were posted up on Brunswick Avenue, a block down from Dee-Dee's Bar and Lounge, with a pair of binoculars glued to their faces waiting for Tamar to arrive. For the past week they had been watching his comings and goings and sometimes would even be able to follow him, if they were lucky. Other times they would somehow get lost in traffic. If Bass didn't know any better, he would have thought Tamar knew he was being followed.

"There he goes right there." Bass pointed to the all-black Cadillac SUV approaching the establishment. Green focused his sights on the truck before rubbing his sweaty hands on his jeans. They watched a massive black guy step out of the bar as the driver of the Cadillac went to the back passenger's door and opened it up. The muscles in Bass's jaws tightened as he watched Tamar's Gator loafer hit the streets. He had to admit, the designer Armani suit Tamar wore fit him perfectly.

"He's an arrogant bastard," Green spoke, snapping Bass from his thoughts. They watched Tamar enter the bar before making their move.

"Come on," Bass ordered and then jumped out of the van. Within seconds, Green was out of the van and by his partner's side, ready to put in work.

The sound of Johnny Taylor played from the old jukebox in the far corner of the bar as Detectives Bass and Green made their way over to the bar to place their order. Once the bartender headed to the end of the bar to fix their drinks, the detectives scanned the room. There was an older couple on the other side of the circular bar counter and a younger guy in the booth by the Private sign hanging over the door in the rear of the room. Once the bartender returned with their drinks, Bass laid a twenty-dollar bill on the counter. "Keep the change." They watched as the bartender rung their order up and took out the change and then placed it in the tip jar. "They probably went behind the door over there," Green tilted his head over to the door sat under the Private sign. He then took a sip of his drink. "So what did you find out about this guy?" Bass took a sip from his drink and frowned.

"Mannn, this shit is strong!" he claimed. Once he sat it back down on the counter, he continued, "My source told me this is the guy that was supplying our friend King before he got himself killed."

"And what else?" Green questioned before taking another gulp of his drink. Bass hunched his shoulders upward.

"Nothing!"

"Nothing?" Green repeated. Before Bass could say another word, they were interrupted by the sound of a deep voice coming from behind them.

"Good afternoon, gentlemen," the voice announced as it made its way closer to the two. Bass and Green turned on their stools and watched Tamar and his two bodyguards approach them.

"Good afternoon," Bass replied, and Green nodded. "You have quite a nice place here." Bass fanned his arm out.

"Thank you. I see you two are enjoying your drinks," Tamar commented, looking down at Green's empty glass.

"Yes, I am," Green responded when he noticed Tamar glancing at the full glass that sat in front of the spot Bass occupied. After raising his wrist to look at the time on his watch, Tamar cleared this throat.

"Well, I hate I can't stay here and chat with you two any longer, but business awaits me elsewhere." Tamar bowed his head and then headed toward the exit. "George," he called out to the bartender over his shoulder, "fix these nice detectives another round on the house."

With that, Tamar and his two bodyguards were out the door. Dumfounded, Bass and Green looked at each other, shocked.

"Come on. Let's go," Bass fumed just as the bartender placed their drinks on the counter. Green watched his partner hurry out the door before he downed both drinks and followed suit. "If we hurry, we can get a tail on him," Bass told his partner once he caught up with him. Tamar had just turned the corner. The detectives made a mad dash for the undercover utility van a block away.

"What's so funny?" Green asked when he noticed Bass suddenly stop in his tracks. "Shit," he cursed when he saw their stakeout van sitting on four flats. There was no way they could call it in since they were on an unofficial stakeout to begin with. "What are you about to do?" Green asked as Bass took out his cell phone and headed down the street.

"There's more than one way to skin a cat," he promised before speaking to the caller that had answered the phone. "You know what favor you owe me. Well, I'm calling in to collect on it." Usually it was Green who would throw all caution to the wind and call in favors from criminals he had occasionally let off the hook.

"That's what I'm talking about," he smiled then followed his partner. Five minutes later, they were hopping in the back of an old Lumina with dark tinted windows.

~ ~ ~

Tamar returned to the bar later on that night with a thousand thoughts running through his mind. Once, he wondered how the two detectives got on his line. He always made sure to cross all his T's and dot all his I's. He knew he had to get to the bottom of things before they became a thorn in his side.

The other thing weighing heavily on his mind was Tawana. He hadn't talked to nor seen her since the night at The Queen's Palace. She had promised to give him a call so they could figure out a time in their schedule to go out to dinner. Tamar was a little confused at how things would go between them. Tawana was like no other woman he had been with. He remembered her coming back into the elite VIP room. She watched lustfully as the two strippers pleased him in every way imaginable. He even saw her pleasing herself as she looked on, and right when he thought she was about to come over and join them, she walked out of the room, leaving him lost and confused. Just the thought of the night at the strip club had Tamar wanting her right then and there. Being that that was impossible, he opted out for the usual. After clapping his hands together twice, the barmaid rounded the bar in his private room. Once he unzipped his pants and released his erection, she got on her knees and assumed the position. "Shit," Tamar cried out from the moistness of her mouth wrapping around his shaft. When she was finished, she wiped her mouth and headed back to her spot behind the bar. Seconds later, his mind was back on how he was going to make his new problems go away. "Get me as much information on those two detectives as you can," he spoke into the receiver of the phone. Tamar listened intently as the person on the other end spoke. "You have twenty-four hours," he shouted, then slammed the phone down on his desk. The long arms of the law were no match for Tamar, and Detectives Bass and Green were just about to see how long they were in the next few days. Tamar marched out of the private room in the basement, where he met up with his bodyguards. After giving them instructions, Tamar walked out also and began to put his plan into motion.

7

"Hadjiiiii," Mya sang out, snapping him from his thoughts.

"What is she doing here?" he asked himself as he looked at the time on his watch. It was a quarter past noon, and usually Mya would have been at the hospital with Sherry. He quickly got up from his favorite recliner and rushed out of his bedroom. He hoped and prayed nothing was wrong with his wife. When he reached the end of the hall, he looked down the stairs, where he spotted Mya along with Lil Sean. Lil Sean had grown so much over the past few years. The older her got, the more he looked like his late father. Hadji wished his cousin Sean could have seen his son before he died. "What's up, Lil Sean?"

"Hey, Uncle Hajjjiii," he giggled, leaving out the *d* in Hadji. Hadji squinted his eyes because he had been trying to get Lil Sean to pronounce his name correctly ever since he was able to talk. Lil Sean jetted from behind his mother's legs and ran into the living room a few feet away.

"Oh no you don't!" Hadji claimed. He then hurried down the steps two at a time before Lil Sean could get a good hiding spot. That was one of Lil Sean's favorite games, hide-n-seek, and he was quite good at it. When Hadji reached the living room entrance, he entered with caution to see if he could hear where Lil Sean was hiding.

"Surprise," Mya cheered, walking up behind him. Hadji slowly made his way across the room over to Sherry, who held Lil Sean on her lap. Speechless, all Hadji could do was lean down and wrap his arms around Sherry and squeeze her tightly.

"I can't breathe," Lil Sean admitted, trying to pry himself from between Sherry and Hadji. When he got loose, he ran over to his mother with his lips poked out.

"Let me look at you," Hadji said once he let Sherry go and took a step back. Sherry did a 360, and even though her head was still bandaged, she was as beautiful as the first day he laid eyes on her at his cousin's beauty salon. All he wanted to do was hold her in his arms so he held her once again. When he looked out the window, his entire body tensed up when he spotted a black four-door Maybach riding toward their home. He knew who it was without seeing who was driving it. Hadji let out a breath of relief when Fuzzy drove into the cul-de-sac and back in the direction she came.

"Hadji, I'm so sorry for . . ." Sherry tried to apologize, but Hadji stepped back and put a finger up to her lips to silence her.

"I love you, babe," he promised, and then kissed her on the lips.

"Well, we have to be going," Mya interrupted their moment. "I'll call you once I finish taking this lil spoiled brat shopping," she told them as her and Lil Sean headed for the front door.

"I hope you feel better, Auntie," Lil Sean yelled out as he headed down the hall with his mother.

"I will," Sherry assured him. "Make sure you get everything you want while you're out," she hollered out, making Mya look back over her shoulder and roll her eyes at her.

"Ay, Mya," Hadji yelled out from the front door just as she fastened Lil Sean in the backseat. When Mya looked up, Hadji was making his way to her truck. By the time he reached the driver's side, Mya was starting the vehicle. "Hadji, I don't know what's up with you and that Fuzzy girl, but you better end it before you lose Sherry," Mya stated in a calm and matter-of-fact voice. Hadji was about to protest, but the look Mya gave him stopped him.

"Damn, she must have saw it too," he thought. Then he reached down into his pocket to give her some money for looking after Sherry while she was in the hospital.

"Don't insult me, Hadji." Mya declined the money he tried to offer her. "Sherry is family. Besides, y'all have always been there for me and Lil Sean," she reminded him, looking into the rearview mirror at her son, who was starting to doze off. She hoped and prayed he did, because then she wouldn't have to take him to the mall, the toy store, and then Chuck E. Cheese's.

"Well at least let me buy Lil Sean something," he offered, sticking his arm further into the truck window for Mya to take the stack of money out of his hand. She knew Hadji wouldn't stop until she took it. She had tried to decline money from him before. Even though Hadji knew Mya had close to a million dollars put away from the robberies him, Sean, and Gee used to do before they got out of the game, he still offered her money. She couldn't ever understand why.

"Don't forget what I said, Hadji!" Mya snatched the money from him and then rolled her eyes at him.

"I got you, cousin," he promised. Then he stepped back from the truck and watched her drive away, before going back into the house.

After peeping his head into the doorway of the living room and finding it empty, Hadji headed upstairs to his bedroom. He stood silently for a few seconds and watched Sherry as she stood in the middle of their room, staring at the picture of them on their special day. Sherry jumped when Hadji walked up on her and wrapped his arms around her and joined her.

"Thank you," she spoke just above a whisper.

"For what?" he asked, confused, never taking his eyes off of the picture.

"For signing the papers stating you didn't want to press charges against me." Hadji stepped back and then turned Sherry around to face him.

"Come on, let's get you in the bath," he insisted. "We'll talk about it later." Hadji took Sherry's hand in his and led her into the master bedroom. Sherry watched as he turned the jets on in the Jacuzzi. "Come here." Sherry did as she was told, and when she was in front of him, Hadji began to undress her, one piece of clothing at a time until she was in her birthday suit. Once she was seated, Hadji undressed himself and did the same.

"I'm so sorry," Sherry apologized with tears in her eyes as she ran her fingers over the old then new bullet scars on his chest. Hadji grabbed her hand and placed it to his lips.

"Shhhh," he demanded and then slid closer to her. Sherry closed her eyes and let the jets massage her body while Hadji lathered the sponge with body wash. When Hadji was finished bathing Sherry, she washed him. It had been so long since they had been in the company of each other. They had never spent a night apart from each other since they had been married, not counting the night he stayed at Fuzzy's place or the nights they stayed laid up in the hospital.

Once they were done, Hadji carried Sherry back into their bedroom and laid her on their bed, where he motioned her down and then tucked her in. They laid side by side in silence, until Sherry turned to face him.

"Hadji," she began. "I don't remember pulling the trigger," she admitted. She had stayed up many nights in the hospital trying to figure out what happened that morning at Fuzzy's place.

"It's okay, babe," Hadji tried comforting her. He wiped the long tears from her cheeks and then kissed the middle of her forehead. Hadji knew Sherry was going through a lot at the time. There were so many questions both of them needed the answers to. "Get some rest. I have a couple of things to check on," he told her as he slid out of bed and walked over to his walk-in closet to find something to put on. Sherry wanted to protest but knew when Hadji had his mind set on doing things, there was no way she could talk him out of it.

"Be careful, Hadji," she whispered. Hadji walked back out of the closet minutes later fully dressed. His heart went out to Sherry as he watched her sitting up in the middle of their bed with her eyes closed in prayer. As much as he hated going out into the streets, he knew he had to, to protect his family. He refused to be the hunted again. This time he was going to be the hunter.

After kissing Sherry on the lips, Hadji headed

downstairs. Once he hopped inside of his NSX and started the engine, he pressed the garage door opener and backed out. He spotted Jamontae and Diontae posted up in a low-key Yukon at the beginning of the cul-de-sac. He saluted the two soldiers as he passed. He had come to respect the goons. Not only were they loyal, but they were also reliable. That made him trust them with his life, as well as his wife's life.

~ ~ ~

On the way to Wilson from Knightdale, Hadji did something he was supposed to have done a few days ago. He called Cee-Cee. "Damn! What a bitch gotta do to get in touch with you?" she scolded after picking up on the second ring. Hadji let her rant on for a few more minutes before he interrupted her.

"Me and my wife got shot."

"What!" Cee-Cee shouted in disbelief. "When? Where? Who?" she asked, not giving Hadji time to answer. Hadji ran down the story of the past few months of his life, at least as much as he could remember.

"Mm-mm-mm." Cee-Cee shook her head from side to side not believing the coincidence.

"What?" Hadji questioned.

"Guess why I been calling you?" she asked. Instead of giving Hadji time to answer, she continued, "I believe I got some valuable information you want." Usually when Cee-Cee had valuable information he wanted, it had something to do with robbing someone, which Hadji had retired from years ago.

"Come on, Cee-Cee. You know I ain't into that lifestyle no more," he reminded her.

"I know, but believe me, Hadji, this is one I know you will be interested in."

"Nah, Cee-Cee. You don't understand. I'm out of that lifestyle," he insisted. That was until she told him who the potential mark was.

"Ant. Gee's flunky. The guy that killed your cousin Sean." To throw a little extra on it she also told him Ant might have been the one who shot him and his wife.

"Give me a few weeks and have everything mapped out for me," he demanded. He then ended the call. Hadji had little time to put a plan together, and the first thing he had to do was going to be the hardest. Hadji scrolled through his call log until he reached the name he was looking for, then pressed send.

"Hello," the caller answered on the first ring.

"Where you at?" Hadji listened as the caller relayed the answer to his question. "Don't move. I'll be there in fifteen minutes," he ordered, then ended the call.

When he pulled into the parking lot of Big Mama's Kitchen, it was packed as usual. Fuzzy spotted Hadji from the surveillance camera as soon as he pulled in. "Excuse me," she spoke politely as she made her way through the restaurant to meet him. She immediately sensed something was wrong when she looked into his face. "Follow me." Fuzzy turned on her heels and headed back to her office so they could talk in private. "What is it?" she asked, taking a seat behind her desk. Hadji closed the door behind him and took the seat in front of her desk before answering.

"I just got word Ant is in New Jersey, and more than likely, so is B.B. and Junior." Just the sound of Hadji mentioning Junior's name got her full attention. "We're taking the trip upstate soon." Though the trip wasn't the one she wanted to take with Hadji, it was one that needed to be taken to get her son back. In a way, Fuzzy wanted to let things between her and B.B. ride since she was Junior's biological mother, but on the other hand, Fuzzy wanted her dead for all the trouble and death she had caused in the midst of getting Junior back. For weeks she had to try to explain to the kids that Junior had to go back home to his mother. It broke Fuzzy's heart to see her daughter cry day and night over her brother.

Her mind was made up. "I'll have the private jet fueled and ready for whenever you give the word," she promised. That was music to Hadji's ears. With only one more thing to do, Hadji stood to his feet.

"I'll call you with the details as soon as I get them." Fuzzy watched Hadji walk across the room to the door. If she could have had things her way, she would've made love to him right then and there, but she couldn't. So instead, she squeezed her legs together tightly and tried her best to control the tingling sensation burning between them.

Hadji breathed a sigh of relief when he turned onto his street and saw Jamontae and Diontae still posted up outside of his place in the Yukon. That relief was replaced with panic when he rode up on the truck to find it empty.

"What the—" Hadji thought, then sped up the driveway and into the garage. When he entered through the side door that led into the kitchen, he saw Jamontae, Diontae, and Sherry at the kitchen table eating dinner.

"Hey, babe," Sherry greeted him between laughter. Jamontae had just finished telling her a joke about him and his brother right before Hadji walked in. She could see the anger in his eyes. "Don't be mad, babe. I asked them to come in because I didn't want to be in here all by myself while you were gone." Hadji looked into her pleading eyes and melted. "Come on and sit down and let me fix you a plate." Sherry watched Hadji take his seat at the head of the table, and then walked over to the stove to fix his plate. By the time she returned, Jamontae had Hadji about to fall out of his seat laughing.

After dinner, Hadji led Jamontae and Diontae out back to the barn, where they shot a few games of pool and went over everything he needed them to do when he went away to New Jersey. "Why we gotta stay back?" Jamontae asked, disappointed they had been put on guard duty once again, away from the action. Hadji was about to answer, until Diontae stepped in.

"Why ask why, nigga?" he asked his brother and then looked at Hadji. "I'm down with whatever you need me to do," he told Hadji, looking him square in his eyes. After giving them strict instructions, Hadji sent them on their way.

Hadji entered the room at the same time Sherry was exiting the shower. "Is everything okay?" she asked, noticing the worried look on his face.

"Come here and let me lotion you down." He waved her over and then walked over to her dresser to retrieve the bottle of cucumber melon lotion. Hadji explained the best way he could he had to leave for a couple of days to handle some business. Sherry didn't like the idea at all, but she knew if she wanted to feel safe again, she would have to allow Hadji to do what he did best: protect them.

After Hadji tucked Sherry into bed, he went into the bathroom to take a long hot shower, hoping to wash away at least a layer of stress. He walked out of the bathroom to find Sherry fast asleep on his side of the bed. He made his way across the room and thought to himself how much he loved and adored his beautiful wife. Before climbing in bed with her, Hadji walked over to the window to close the curtains. A smile spread across his face when he glanced down and spotted Jamontae and Diontae posted up in the Yukon. He had told them to take off for a couple of days until he got ready to take his trip, but he guessed they insisted on keeping an eye on things. Hadji gave them a salute, and to his surprise, the dome light in the truck came on, which gave him a clear view of them when they saluted back to him. It was at that point Hadji made up his mind to promote them as soon as he got back from New Jersey.

8

It took Crystal a week before she finally decided to give Jay a call. She was expecting him to call her first, but he never did. That only made her more curious to find out who he really was. He had proven to be different because usually when she gave a guy her number, he called her within a day or two, if not the same day. "Oh well," she thought when she got his voicemail. No sooner than she hung up, her phone was ringing. She looked at the caller ID and saw it was Jay calling her back. She didn't know why, but for some strange reason she felt butterflies in her stomach. She hadn't felt that way since . . . Her mind trailed off to her ex, Menace. The only man to capture her heart completely.

"Hello," she quickly answered after the third ring, not wanting to miss his call.

"Hola, my beautiful jewel," Jay greeted in a thick Spanish accent. "Are you there?" he asked after a brief moment of silence. "Are we gonna sit on the phone having a breathing contest or are you going to let me take you out for dinner?" Jay joked, breaking the ice.

Crystal thought long and hard before she answered.

"Only if I can choose the place," she insisted, since she knew nothing about the mysterious man on the other end of the phone.

"Of course," he replied. After giving Jay the address to the restaurant they would be dining at for the afternoon, she ended the call.

"You sure are happy today," Tawana announced from the doorway, looking at Crystal through the reflection of her mirror.

"Maybe it's because I just got off the phone with Jay," she replied and then turned around. Tawana squeezed and then ran across the room to get the scoop on Crystal's new friend.

"So what's up with him?" Tawana asked excitedly.

"He's taking me out to dinner this afternoon," she admitted. Tawana looked down at her sister like she was crazy. "I chose the place!" she stressed when she noticed the crazed look in her sister's eyes. Their rule had always been to choose the place when it came to dealing with someone they didn't know. Whether it was business or pleasure.

"That's my big sis," Tawana teased.

"Bitch, I'm the one that made the rules," she cursed Tawana, then rolled her eyes. They both laughed as Tawana started putting Crystal's hair up in a tight bun. They talked a little more until they were interrupted by the sound of Junior calling out Tawana's name.

"Hold up, baby. Mommy will be right there," she answered, putting the finishing touches on Crystal's 'do. "There!" Crystal looked into the mirror and had to admit she was looking like a pure diva.

"Thanks, girl." Tawana waved her off then headed for the door. "Wait! Before you leave, which one?" Crystal ran into her closet and seconds later returned with two outfits.

Tawana looked from one outfit to the other with a finger pressed up against her lips. "That one," she pointed to the sexy black Chanel dress with the back out. Crystal looked at the dress and frowned doubtfully. "Trust me," Tawana winked before disappearing from her room to go check on her son.

"The black dress it is." She threw her shoulders

upward and then headed to the bathroom to get herself together.

After getting dressed, Crystal looked at herself in the mirror in admiration. The dress fit her like a glove. The only concern she had was she was overdressed for the dinner date. Then again, reflecting back to the day she first met Jay, she prayed she wasn't the one that would be underdressed for the occasion. "Maybe I should have chosen the Christian Dior pant set," she thought, turning around and looking at the reflection of her shapely rear. Pressed for time, Crystal grabbed the matching handbag and her keys off of the dresser and then headed downstairs.

"Hey, Aunt Chris, you look pretty," Junior cheered as he dropped the cookie he was eating on the table in front of him and ran over to hug her.

"Hold on, Junior." She dodged his hug by stepping to the side.

"Come here, Junior. You don't want to get chocolate all over Auntie's dress, do you?" Tawana said. Junior held out his messy hands and then licked them.

"They're clean now, Mommy, see!" Junior held his

hands in the air to show Tawana and Crystal they were now clean. Tawana looked over at Crystal and shook her head before wiping Junior's hands clean.

"Let Auntie give her handsome nephew a kiss instead," Crystal offered. She leaned down and planted a kiss on top of Junior's head. Junior blushed and then made his way back over to his seat at the table and stuffed his mouth full of cookies. Tawana stared at her big sister with pride. This would mark the first official date Crystal had been on since Menace's death. Well at least the first serious date. "So, how do I look?" she asked, She did a 360 to give Tawana a view from all angles. Tawana was at a loss for words. "I knew I should have worn the pant set," Crystal pouted and headed to the doorway to head back upstairs to her room to change before it was too late.

"NO!" Tawana shouted, stopping Crystal in her tracks. "You look beautiful," she admitted. Crystal looked into her sister's eyes to see if she was pulling her leg.

"You think he'll like it?"

"He'd be a fool not to," she responded with furrowed brows. Crystal relaxed and made her way back over to

Tawana. "Go get 'em, girl." Crystal gave her sister a weak smile followed by a kiss on the cheek, and then made her way out the side door of the kitchen that led to the garage where her recently purchased Cadillac SLR sat.

"Come on, Lil Man. Time to go to bed," Tawana informed her son once he finished his snack.

"Awww, Ma. Do I have to?" he pouted. Tawana almost melted when she turned around and looked into his puppy-dog eyes.

"Yes, Junior, because we have a big day ahead of us tomorrow, remember?" Junior's eyes lit up remembering the promise Tawana made to him about taking him to Dave & Buster's. Every chance she got, they did something together since his return. She felt like she had a lot of making up to do for the lost time she had missed out on when Junior was away.

"Yayyyyy," he cheered, clapping his hands together as he jumped up and down in place. Tawana placed her hand on top of his head and guided him out of the kitchen and into the hallway. As they took the stairs to the second floor, Junior asked Tawana if he could sleep with her. "Of course you can." She smiled, bypassing his room. When they reached her bedroom door, Junior took off across the room and dived on top of her bed.

"Come on, Mommy." He waved her over with the comforter pushed back, patting the spot reserved for her. Tawana did as she was told, and when she was situated, Junior tucked her in. She watched him lean over toward the nightstand and touch the lamp shade twice, dimming it down a few notches. "Goodnight, Mommy," he yawned with his tiny hand over his mouth.

"Goodnight, Speedy," she responded before she knew it.

"I'm not Speedy, Mommy. I'm Junior," her son replied.

"I know, baby." Tawana rolled to her left and planted a kiss on top of Junior's sleepy head. Then she looked up at the ceiling like she did most nights when she couldn't sleep. She reminisced of the good times she and Junior's father shared over the years, until she managed to doze off.

~ ~ ~

Crystal silently opened one of the double doors to the mansion and slid between the crack. She prayed she

111

would be able to slip past the kitchen area without being noticed. She peeped her head through the door and observed Tawana along with Junior, sitting at the island in the middle of the kitchen eating breakfast. She debated joining them, but to avoid the million and one questions, not to mention the cursing out Tawana was sure to lay on her, she swiftly made her way to the other side of the door and down the hallway.

Crystal breathed a sigh of relief and closed the door behind her once she made it to her room. She walked over to the vanity and looked in the mirror at her reflection. She had to admit that not only did she look vibrant, but she also felt alive again for the first time in her life since she lost Menace. Not a day had gone by that she didn't think of Menace, not until she met Jay. Just the thought of the mystery man brought a smile to her face. She was so lost thinking about the past day they had being in each other's company, that she didn't even notice Tawana had opened the door and entered. "You scared me," Crystal admitted with her hand over her heart.

"Why didn't you answer your phone?" she asked, storming across the room. "Better yet, why did you turn your phone off? You had me worried half to death!" she shouted, now standing in Crystal's face. When Tawana paused long enough for Crystal to respond, she answered each question one at a time.

"Tawana, I'm sorry for not answering the call. My intentions were to call you back, but I was having so much fun I lost track of time." Tawana softened when she saw something in Crystal's eyes she hadn't seen in a very long time. "And the reason I turned my phone off was because Ant's stupid ass kept calling me and I didn't want Jay to think anything."

"You really like him, don't you?" Tawana asked, already knowing the answer. When she got no answer, she smiled. "So, tell me all about your date." Tawana squeezed like a teenager, ready to hear all of the juicy details. Crystal went on to tell Tawana about how instead of eating at the restaurant she had previously chosen for them, Jay insisted they eat at a much more exquisite location since she was too beautiful not to show off. From the frown on Tawana's face, Crystal could tell she wasn't pleased with the news. "You know the rule, Crystal. Never let them pick the place." Crystal held her head down because she knew she was wrong for going against their rule, especially without letting Tawana know the change of plans first. "Go ahead," Tawana instructed, not meaning to be so hard on her sister. "Where did y'all go?" Crystal continued her story. Tawana was quite impressed to hear Jay owned an exclusive restaurant in upper New Jersey. Crystal went on to tell her about how after dinner they ended up at Jay's estate in Jersey City.

"I'm telling you, girl, the nigga's shit is bigger than ours. He got to be doing some other shit," she shouted out. Before she could go any further, she was interrupted by the ringing of her cell phone. She quickly pressed Ignore when she saw Ant's name pop up on the display screen. "Damn Ant is so worrisome," Crystal claimed. She then turned around and placed her cell phone on the charger. "What?" Crystal asked when she turned around and noticed the grin on Tawana's face.

"Auntie! Auntie!" Junior screamed as he ran into the room and jumped into Crystal's arms. "You coming with us to Dave & Buster's?" he asked after planting a big wet juicy kiss on her cheek. After returning his wet kisses, Crystal sat Junior down and broke the news to him.

"Auntie can't this time. I have some business to attend to." Junior poked his lips out and looked down at the floor. "But," Crystal said excitedly, hoping to cheer her nephew up. She hated to disappoint him. "Auntie will take you to the amusement park this weekend. How does that sound to you?" Junior quickly lifted his head and showed off his missing tooth smile.

"Yayyyy," Junior cheered as he jumped up and down clapping his hands. "You hear, Mommy! Auntie gonna take me to the amusement park!"

"I heard her," Tawana replied as she looked at Crystal to assure her she was going to make sure she kept her word to Junior. "Come, Junior. It's time to go to Dave & Buster's." Junior took off out of the room as quick as possible to go get his jacket. Tawana smiled as she looked into her sister's eyes. "Be careful," she warned, and then hugged her neck.

"I will," Crystal replied, and then let her go. Crystal watched Tawana make her way out of the room before she headed to her walk-in closet to find something to wear. When she came out, she was greeted by the sound of her ringing cell phone. After letting it go to voicemail, it beeped, indicating she had just received a text. It was from Ant, letting her know he needed her to meet him at the spot in an hour. She texted back, "OK," and then got dressed. Twenty minutes later, she was headed out the door.

~ ~ ~

Crystal let out a sigh of relief when she spotted an empty parking space behind Ant's Range Rover, which was parked directly in front of the spot. It was a tight fit, but after a few adjustments, she made the snug fit. "I know this nigga didn't," she cursed when she looked inside of his truck and spotted a female sitting in the passenger seat, on her phone. She was so busy texting, she never noticed Crystal eyeing her, nor the frown that was plastered on her face. "I got a word or two for his ass." Crystal spun around on her heels and rushed to the door. She was so anxious to get into the house and give Ant a piece of her mind, she damn near broke the key off in the key cylinder.

When she stepped into the living room where Ant was comfortably sitting on the couch, she noticed him texting as well. "I know this nigga ain't," she thought as she stood over him with her hands on her hips. Ant looked up after putting his phone away.

"So, where you been ever since yesterday?" he asked with an attitude. "I been trying to reach you."

"It ain't none of your damn business where I been. You need to be concerned about your little bitch in the car." Ant stood to his feet and smiled. He could see Crystal was bothered by Chelsea being there with him. That was the main reason for bringing her.

"Jealous?" he asked, rubbing it in.

"Psst! Please! That bitch ain't got nothing on me." She waved him off and then headed to the back room. "What in the fuck did you want anyway?" Ant followed behind Crystal, watching her ass bounce with each step she took. Instead of answering, he let her figure it out for herself. Crystal opened up the safe and immediately knew it was short.

"That's what I was hitting you up for," he said once she turned around and looked him in his face. She was about to go in on him until he let her know he had straightened everything out. "I had to fire one of the crew last night after Ashley told me she saw Raheem stashing money in his pocket when he thought no one was looking.

Ashley was young, cold-hearted, and ruthless. She was also one of the most thorough female members of their crew. That's why they choose her spot to set up shop in. She had proven her loyalty on more than one occasion.

"That's my girl." Crystal smiled, proud of her young protege. She had personally recruited her when they first moved to New Jersey from North Carolina when King first stepped on the scene. If it wasn't for Ashley filling King in on the move the neighborhood jack boys were about to hit him with, he would've died the first month he arrived. "So where is Raheem?" Crystal asked, mad he still had his life. The look Ant gave her answered it all, but his next words sealed it.

"Ask Ashley!" he answered with a raised brow. Crystal made a mental note to give Ashley a call when she left, to get the full details on what she did with Raheem. She didn't want anything to come back and bite them in the ass. "Well it seems like you got everything under control, so I'm going to be headed back home." Crystal walked past Ant, slightly brushing her breast against his chest. She hated to admit it, but his body felt good, so good. She opened her eyes and exhaled as she walked back into the living room. Before she forgot, she turned to address Ant about the female he had in his truck, but he beat her to the punch.

"On the real, Chris; next time you need to answer your phone when I call you. The next time it could be a real emergency," he said seriously. Crystal knew he was right, so she didn't put up much of a fight with him.

"You're right." Ant looked at Crystal confused. For a second he thought she had gone soft on him. "And for the record, if you bring that bitch back to my spot, I'ma bust you and her shit," Crystal said seriously and then opened the door. Ant didn't push his luck because he knew she meant what she had just said to him and he had personally seen the kind of work she was capable of putting in. Before she made it out the door, Ant's phone rang. "Oh, ain't nobody, babe. I'm on my way out right now." Crystal slammed the door behind her and made it down the steps just in time to see the female ending the call. They locked eyes for a brief moment, but that was all it took. From that day forth, she was on Crystal's radar.

"Damn, that bitch look familiar," she said as she

started the engine to her Cadillac. She was going to find out who Ant's new chick was if it was the last thing she did, and she knew just who could help her. Crystal picked up her cell and dialed a number.

"Hello," the caller answered on the second ring.

"What's up, Ashley? I need for you to find out as much as you can about Ant's new chick," Crystal replied.

"Already on it," Ashley answered and then ended the call. A victorious smile crossed Crystal's face knowing in a matter of time, she would have everything she needed to know about Ant's new friend.

9

Detective Bass and his partner Detective Green, along with the Trenton Narcotic SWAT Team sat in unmarked cars up and down Brunswick Avenue, watching the comings and goings of the patrons of Dee-Dee's Bar. Detective Bass smiled openly because that was the day he planned to get his payback on Tamar for humiliating him the last time they ran into each other. "Yo' ass is mine today," he said to himself as he looked down at the search warrant in his hand. He did everything by the book this time, so he planned to shine bright.

"Here he comes," he heard the head SWAT leader announce through the walkie-talkie that sat between him and his partner.

"You ready?" Green asked, looking over at Bass.

"No doubt," he replied as they both watched Tamar pull up in front of the bar. Just the sight of Tamar being escorted into the bar like he was the president or a high-up official made Bass's blood boil. Once they were inside, Bass and the SWAT Team crept toward the front door. "Three, two, one," Bass signaled with his fingers. He followed behind as the Narc Team rushed into the building with their weapons drawn.

"EVERYBODY, DOWN ON THE FLOOR!" the SWAT leader demanded. Everyone in the area did as they were told.

"What the—" Tamar mouthed as he looked at the security monitor on his desk as he watched his business get raided. He knew it was only a matter of minutes before they made their way down to his private office in the basement. Lucky for him, he had not sent his personal barmaid next door, through the secret passageway, to retrieve Tawana's order.

"What do you want us to do, boss?" one of his bodyguards asked with his gun in hand.

"Stand down," he answered lifting his hand high. "They got nothing on us and they will find nothing," Tamar assured. He never kept drugs in the building, and the weapons they had were registered. Both guards holstered their guns and took a seat and waited for SWAT's arrival. Thirty seconds later the basement door came crashing down.

"Hands where I can see them," the SWAT leader ordered. Tamar raised his hands high with a huge smile on his face, looking down at the red beams covering the front of his shirt.

"Welcome," he greeted as Detectives Bass and Green came into the room. "Would you two like your usual drinks?" Tamar asked, looking from Bass to Green. "Vodka and Red Bull?" he nodded to Green, remembering his drink of choice. Bass stormed over to the table Tamar sat at and then slammed his hands-on top of it and leaned forward so he was face-to-face with him while SWAT retrieved the guards' weapons.

"I can't wait to see that smug-ass smile disappear from your face when the judge gives your black ass life," Bass threatened with spit spewing from his mouth. You could hear weapons being cocked as Tamar reached into his shirt pocket and pulled out a handkerchief before wiping his face.

"Is this how you treat the tax-paying citizens of Trenton?" he asked after placing his handkerchief on the table between him and Bass. Bass ran his arm across the table, knocking the handkerchief and everything else on top of the table onto the floor. As the two bodyguards snickered, Green walked over to the one closest to him and hit him in his mouth. Bass turned around as the bodyguard jumped to his feet to defend himself, who was immediately taken down by Green and three other SWAT members.

"Sorry," Green apologized to Bass. "It looked like he was going for a weapon," he lied, knowing they had secured their guns. Bass smiled and then turned his attention back to Tamar, who still seemed to be unfazed by the raid. "I got you, you black son of bitch! You won't get off as easily as your old friend Mr. King," Bass promised. A smile slowly crept to his face once he saw the smile leave Tamar's after mentioning King's name, so to add on, he revealed a little secret he had been keeping for a while. "We got someone in your camp that's willing to testify!" It was then that Tamar felt like someone had slapped him in his face. Satisfied, Bass took a step back and ordered for SWAT to get them out of there and search the entire place from top to bottom. Tamar stood up with confidence and then turned around so Bass could cuff him. On the way out to the paddy wagon,

Tamar's mind raced with thoughts of who could have turned state on him. The first thing he was going to do was call Tawana and give her the heads-up and get her to look into things for him. Until then, he would keep his mouth shut and pray Bass was bluffing.

~ ~ ~

Tawana couldn't believe her eyes as Bo pulled the Bentley truck over a couple of blocks up from Dee-Dee's Bar and Lounge. She watched Detective Bass personally escort Tamar into the back of the paddy wagon along with his two bodyguards and the bartender. "Damn," Bo cursed in disbelief.

"This can't be good," Tawana added. "A few minutes earlier and we would've been right along with them." Just the thought of being taken away from Junior gave her the chills. She was about to order Bo to make a U-turn, until something, or rather a thought, came to mind. After dialing a number, Tawana told Bo to take her back home. "I need a favor," she said into the cell phone when the caller answered the phone.

~ ~ ~

"You bullshitting," Crystal shouted after Tawana

relayed the news of Tamar's arrest.

"I wish I was!" Tawana replied sadly. She hated to admit it, but she was beginning to get a soft spot for Tamar. She thought by not calling him after the night he came to the strip club everything would go back to normal, but she was wrong. At the meeting today, she was going to tell him how she was feeling, but now she would have to wait while she figured out a way to get him out of jail. Her thoughts were interrupted by the ringing of her cell phone. After checking the display screen, she immediately answered. "So, what's the deal?" she asked. Then she waited patiently for Mrs. Battle to give her the 411.

Melonie Battle was Tawana's personal attorney. She was one of the best in the state. Not only did she have the connections in the Trenton Police Department, but in the FBI as well, due to the fact that her father was deep in the system when he was alive. Melonie was the reason King stayed on top for so long when he was still living.

"Okay. When the paperwork is complete, tell him to call me immediately," she told her. Before Tawana ended the call, she had to laugh at her friend. "Yes, that one is off-limits." After sharing a hearty laugh, she ended the call. "What?" Tawana asked Crystal when she turned around and looked in her face.

"So, Tamar's off-limits now?" she questioned. "That's what I'm talking about. Claim your man," Crystal teased by snapping her fingers and snaking her neck.

Tawana rolled her eyes and said, "Well, I guess the old saying is true." Crystal stopped laughing and looked at her sister confused. "You can take the chick out of the hood, but will never be able to take the hood out of the chick." After realizing what Tawana had just said, Crystal stuck her middle finger up and turned to leave the room.

"Call me when your man get out of jail," she teased, and then headed up to her room. Tawana sat at the island in the kitchen and thought about Tamar and where their future together could lead. Her thoughts were interrupted when Junior skipped into the kitchen and called out her name.

"MOMMY," he shouted, scarring her half to death. By instinct, Tawana reached for her handbag which contained her baby 9 mm Glock.

"Hi, baby. What are you doing sneaking up on

Mommy like that?" she asked, removing her hand from her bag. Ignoring her question, he asked one of his own.

"When can I go visit my sister and cousin again?" Junior's question caught Tawana totally by surprise even though she knew it would come up again sooner than later since he had asked the same question before. She hated to lie to her son, but she knew what she was about to say was for the best.

"It won't be long now. I talked to your sister and she said her mother said she will be to get you real soon, once she finishes handling some important business."

"Yayyyyy," Junior cheered. He then turned around and skipped out of the kitchen and headed back up to his room to finish playing with his new toys Tawana had purchased him the day before.

After she wiped the tears that had trickled down her face, a voice spoke up from behind her. "You can't keep lying to that chile," Mrs. Deloris said disapprovingly to Tawana. She constantly told her not to lie to Junior because he would eventually resent her for it in the long run, if or once everything came out. Even though she knew Mrs. Deloris was right, Tawana spoke her peace.

"Please, Mrs. Thompson, not right now." Tawana stood up from her seat and headed to the refrigerator to fix herself a glass of apple juice. When she made it back to her seat, Mrs. Deloris was seated in the chair in front of her. To Tawana's surprise, Mrs. Deloris didn't pry any further.

"So, have you called Melonie to check up on Tamar?" Mrs. Deloris asked, catching Tawana by surprise once again.

"How did you—" Tawana began to ask until Mrs. Deloris cut her off.

"I know everything that goes on in them streets, chile. Did you forget I use to run them myself?" she asked in a matter-of-fact tone.

"She should be down there right now," Tawana answered, and then took a sip from her glass.

"Good," Mrs. Deloris smiled, glad to see Tawana was on top of her job. They sat for the better part of an hour before Crystal came back downstairs with her handbag draped over her shoulder.

"And where are you on your way to?" Mrs. Deloris asked with an accusing smile on her face.

"Out with my new friend." Crystal blushed and then looked away to avoid Mrs. Deloris seeing the excitement in her eyes.

"New friend?" Mrs. Deloris asked with a raised brow. "Does Anthony know about this new friend?" Mrs. Deloris asked, making Tawana let out a light chuckle. Crystal shot her eyes in her sister's direction before turning to address Mrs. Deloris.

"Ant is not my man nor my concern. You should be asking the girl he had outside the spot waiting in the car for him when I met with him earlier." Crystal's last comment caught everyone by surprise.

"He took a female to the spot?" Tawana asked, not believing her ears. Without waiting for Crystal to answer, Tawana took out her cell phone and dialed Ant's number. It went straight to voicemail. After two more tries, she left a message for him to call her back as soon as possible.

"Well, I must be going. My ride is out front," Crystal announced after looking at the text Jay had just sent her.

"Tell Jay I said hello," Tawana called out behind her sister.

"Jay," Mrs. Deloris said out loud but to herself.

Tawana looked over at the confused look on Mrs. Deloris's face. Before she could ask what was wrong, Mrs. Deloris was on her way to the front door. By the time Tawana caught up with her, they saw the chauffeur escorting Crystal into the back of the stretched Hummer. "Jesus," Mrs. Deloris whispered as she watched the Hummer pull off from the estate.

"You know him?" Tawana asked, shocked. Instead of answering Tawana's question, Mrs. Deloris just gave her a wink and then turned around and made her way back into the mansion. "Who is this woman?" Tawana asked herself as she watched Mrs. Deloris disappear down the hallway.

~ ~ ~

Tawana put Junior to bed and headed downstairs to the kitchen to fix her a late-night snack. "Can't sleep, huh?" she asked Mrs. Deloris, who was at the stove brewing a fresh pot of tea.

"Do I ever?" she responded, looking back over her shoulder. Tawana shook her head from side to side as she made her way over to the table to take a seat. After fixing them both a cup, Mrs. Deloris joined her. "So, have you talked to Tamar?" she asked after taking her first sip. Tawana dropped her shoulders and let out a long sigh of dread.

"Yeah. He's out. He said he was getting away for a while and he would get in touch with me once things cool off." They both sat in silence, thinking the same thing. Tawana was the first to break the silence and speak on it. "Who in the world can supply the demand I need?" she asked more to herself. When she looked up, Mrs. Deloris had a huge smile on her face. "What are you smiling at?"

"The answer is right under your nose and you don't even see it," Mrs. Deloris answered. "Jay and his brother have all the work you need." Tawana bobbed her head up and down. She knew there was something about Jay, but she couldn't put her finger on it. Now she knew why. He was too connected.

"I'll see what I can do," she told Mrs. Deloris before her mind drifted off to a much more important problem she may be facing. She still had no clue who the informant was nor if they were in her crew or Tamar's. After looking at her watch, Tawana took one last sip of her tea and then stood to her feet. She had to leave for the club early since Crystal had called her and said she would be running late. Tawana hoped she brought Jay along with her because they really needed to get their hands on some more product, and fast.

"Go on ahead, chile. Junior's safe with me." Mrs. Deloris smiled and waved her off.

"Thank you." Tawana blew Mrs. Deloris a kiss before rushing off to her bedroom to get herself together. There was only one more thing she had to do when she got upstairs to her room. It was something she knew had to be done. She took out the card she'd taken a few weeks ago and then dialed the number written on it. The caller answered on the second ring. "Hi. May I speak to Detective Bass?" she asked in her most polite voice.

10

"So have you heard anything from any of your sources?" Bo asked Tawana as she sat at her desk in deep thought. Bo was truly concerned about his boss's well-being.

"Nah. Not a thing," she admitted, looking up into his eyes. She had not felt that vulnerable since the day Junior was taken away from her. That was a feeling she vowed never to feel again. That's why she was so determined to terminate the rat problem as soon as possible. Bo watched Tawana as she stood to her feet and walked across the room and began to stare down at the crowd in the strip club. "As soon as things start to go right for me, something always happens that changes everything. I can't leave her like this."

"Leave who like what?" Bo asked, confused. The moment the words came out of Tawana's mouth, she regretted saying them. She was waiting for the right time to tell Bo she was getting out of the game and turning everything over to Crystal at the end of the year.

"Bo, I'm quitting the game in a few months," she admitted without taking her eyes off the crowd. She knew the news of her exit really hurt him and she couldn't bear to look back into his eyes. If she did, she was bound to break down. "Don't worry. When I do, you and Mrs. Deloris will be well taken care of." She was hoping her reply would soften the impact of the bomb she had just dropped on him, but she was wrong.

"I'm not worried about being taken care of, B.B. I'm worried about who's gonna take care of you and Junior!" he said a little louder than normal. Tawana was about to turn around, until she spotted Crystal walking into the club. What really threw her off was when she spotted a Hispanic male by her side. "Um, excuse me for a second, Bo. We'll discuss this later." Without waiting for his response, Tawana walked around Bo and headed downstairs to greet Crystal and Jay, or Jesus as Mrs. Deloris called him.

After several minutes of greeting patrons and dissing stalkers, Tawana approached the VIP booth her sister and Jay were seated at. Before she was able to get within ten feet of them, Tawana was stopped by Jay's two bodyguards. "If you don't want to ruin that nice suit you're wearing, I suggest you don't put a fucking finger on her," Bo threatened the bodyguard that was about to attempt to frisk Tawana.

"B.B.," Jay called out to her and smiled. "Come join us." Jay's bodyguard moved to the side to let Tawana pass while never taking his eyes off of Bo. As Tawana made her way over to take a seat across from them at the booth, she took in Jay's attire. She had to admit, he was kind of sexy for a Hispanic man, and with the custom-made pinky ring that adorned his left hand, she knew he was about his business. King was about to get the same exact ring before he got killed. "You have a nice place here," Jay spoke and then bowed his head gracefully.

"Thank you. I take it you are enjoying yourself?" she asked.

"I am," he answered with Crystal wrapped tightly in his arms. To Tawana's surprise, Crystal leaned in closer and kissed him on his cheek.

"I hear you got a little problem," Jay stated in a serious tone, throwing Tawana off balance. She quickly shot Crystal an unpleased look that let her know she wasn't happy about her loose lips to her "new friend." She was definitely going to deal with her later on, but for now, Tawana had a few questions of her own.

"So, Jesus," Tawana began, letting him know she knew who he was and what he was about.

"I see you do your homework as well, B.B." Jay smiled approvingly.

"I do," she admitted.

"Good. Well then, you should know I have the best product, as well as price, around." Jay sat and waited for her response, but she gave none. "But, we will get to all of that once you take care of the little problem in your crew," Jay said before sitting back in the booth to look into her eyes to see if he could get a good read on them.

"That will be terminated very soon," she assured him. Satisfied, Jay leaned forward and grabbed his wine glass.

"Well, let's toast." Tawana and Crystal picked up their glasses and joined. "To a new beginning," Jay cheered.

"To a new beginning," Tawana and Crystal cheered. The threesome downed their champagne at the same time.

"Well, I have to be going, my love," Jay announced, looking over at Crystal.

"So soon?" she pouted. Jay reached over and put his finger under her chin before placing is lips on hers.

"I have a busy day ahead of me tomorrow," he admitted. Crystal was just about to kiss him again, until he leaned back and suggested, "Unless you want to join me on my trip to Miami?"

"Jay, don't play with me," Crystal said, looking up at him.

"Well, if you have other plans." Crystal looked up at Tawana pleadingly. "Yes, I'll go," she answered after Tawana assured her she would handle things in her absence. They all stood and said their goodbyes. Before Jay could make his exit, Tawana stopped him.

"How did you know my name was B.B.? Only the streets call me by name."

Jay smiled his million-dollar smile and then answered, "B.B., I am the streets!" After giving her a wink, Jay wrapped his arm around Crystal's waist and headed out of the strip club.

From the booth on the far side of the club, Ant watched Crystal and Jay make their way out the exit. "What's the matter, babe?" Chelsea asked, noticing Ant's body tense up.

"It ain't nothing," he assured her before looking back up at the stripper in front of them, peeling off a few more bills from the stack of money on the table and tossing them on her. "Come on, let's go." Without another word, Ant grabbed his jacket off the back of the booth and hurried toward the door.

"What's wrong with him?" Chelsea asked herself as she gathered the rest of the money from the table and followed suit. They made it out of the club just as Jay's stretched Hummer pulled out of the lot. Once Chelsea saw Ant's attention on the big black truck, a smile came to her face. Since she had been kicking it with Ant, his lips had become very loose in the bedroom, and Chelsea had learned before he got deep into the drug game with someone by the name of B.B., he used to be a stick-up kid. "So, is Jay someone of interest now?" she asked. The thought of all the money they could possibly come up on crossed her mind and made her love box throb.

"You know that cat?" he asked, surprised as he watched the taillights disappear in the distance. When he turned and looked down at her, he noticed a glow on her face.

"What?" she asked, taking a step closer before pressing her lips against his. "Who doesn't know Jesus, the drug God?" she answered, and then turned and headed for Ant's Range Rover parked in his VIP parking space beside the entrance. Ant watched Chelsea sashay her phat ass to the driver's door. The sound of her disarming the alarm brought him back to the present.

"I'ma fuck the shit out of her tonight," he said to himself as he adjusted his erection and walked over to the passenger side and hopped in.

"And I can't wait for you to tear this pussy up," Chelsea admitted. Ant laughed on the outside, but inside he made a mental note to watch what he said out loud around her because it could be detrimental to his health. After jotting down Jay's tag number, he reached over and began rubbing Chelsea's thigh as she drove them home.

"You gonna fuck around and have a nigga fall in love with yo' ass," Ant admitted when he realized she wasn't wearing any panties.

"You sound like that's a bad thing," she replied, taking her eyes off the road for a second to look in his direction. Instead of responding, Ant slid his finger deep inside her love tunnel, making a soft moan escape her mouth. Chelsea damn near came when Ant removed his finger and licked her juices clean from them.

From the moment they stepped out of the Range Rover, to the time they stepped foot inside the condo, Ant and Chelsea were all over each other. Their lust-filled night ended at five o'clock that morning in the jacuzzi. After drying each other off, they headed to the bedroom and cuddled between the sheets. Chelsea made small talk, but Ant's mind was in another place. All he could think about was Jesus and a way to get what he had. Maybe then, Crystal would notice his true potential. "Mmmmm," Ant relaxed when he felt Chelsea's warm mouth devour his manhood. "Damn, I love you, girl," he promised. "What's wrong?" he asked when she removed him from her mouth.

"What did you say?"

"You heard me," he answered, looking deep into her eyes. Chelsea's eyes began to water as she returned his stare. It broke her heart she couldn't love him the way he loved her, because her heart belonged to one man, and one man only.

"I love you too," she stroked his ego as he wiped her tears away. "It will all be over soon," Chelsea coached herself as Ant placed his hand on the top of her head and guided it back down South. She placed him back in her mouth and did what she did best: take him to ecstasy. Thirty minutes later, Ant was out like a light. As Ant snuggled next to her, Chelsea took out her cell phone and began to text. "Everything is a go." A smile spread across her face five minutes later when she received a reply letting her know he would call her in the morning and put a plan together. Satisfied, Chelsea deleted the text and then powered off her phone. Before lying down, she planted a kiss on Ant's lips. She hated that things had to go down the way they were going, but there was no other way. Lines had been crossed and someone had to pay.

~ ~ ~

A week had passed and Crystal had yet to return to New Jersey. If it wasn't for the fact that she had been calling at least twice a day, Tawana would have been worried. That and Jay promised to have the information on the inside informant for her in the next couple of days. That was two days ago. While she waited on her sister's return, she passed her time by taking Detective Bass up on his offer and going out on a few dates with him. During their dinner dates, she tried to get as much information out of him as she could without being too obvious.

Tawana looked at her watch and noticed she only had about thirty minutes before she had to head out to meet Detective Bass if she wanted to be on time. She was going to make him wait, but time wasn't on her side and she needed answers quick.

After getting herself together, Tawana grabbed her handbag and headed downstairs. When she reached the bottom of the stairs, she smiled. She could hear Mrs. Deloris and Junior in the kitchen laughing. Tawana looked into the kitchen and spotted Junior with a cookie in his hand, flying it toward Mrs. Deloris's open mouth like he was flying it into a tunnel. "Zmmmmm," he made the sound as Mrs. Deloris bit the cookie in half. Junior giggled louder and then took the other half into his mouth and did the same. Tawana turned and headed toward the front door before either of them spotted her.

As soon as she reached for the door latch, her cell phone began to vibrate. It was the call she had been waiting on. "What you got for me?" she asked Jay with a smile on her face. After revealing then information he got from his reliable source down at the Trenton Police Department, her smile slowly faded. "Are you sure?" she asked. After assuring Jay the rat would be terminated before his return, he assured her he would be ready to do business. Tawana ended the call and took a deep breath before pulling the door open. She slowly removed her designer shades from her bag and slid them over her eyes.

"What's up, boss lady?" Bo greeted her with the back door to the Bentley truck open, waiting for her to enter.

"Hey, Bo," she replied as she made her way down the steps. When she got into the back of the truck, he closed the door behind her and jumped in the driver's seat.

"Where to?" he asked as he pulled off from the estate.

"Hold on. Let me find out." Tawana took out her cell phone and then cursed.

"What's wrong? Did you forget something?" Bo asked, ready to make a U-turn and head back to the house.

"You don't have to go back. My phone just died," she replied, digging in her handbag for her car charger. Coming up empty, she asked to use his phone. After unlocking it, Bo handed it back to her. Tawana blocked the number and then called Detective Bass to find out the location of their dinner date. He answered on the second ring.

"Hello," he answered on the way to his car.

"Hey, you," Tawana spoke into the cell. Bass's face lit up like a Christmas tree when he heard Tawana's voice. He hurried himself inside his car before his wife came out the door bitching. Ever since he had got caught cheating a few months back, their marriage had been on the rocks. To make matters even worse, their sex life was now nonexistent. He hoped that would change after today, because he intended on bedding Tawana later after dinner.

"I'm on my way too." Bass paused to think of a restaurant near an exclusive hotel.

"There's been a change of plan," she interrupted. "Meet me at The Queen's Palace in twenty minutes." Before Bass could reply, Tawana ended the call. Bo looked into the rearview mirror at his Boss and smiled because he knew how in control she needed to be of every situation she was in. Bo didn't like the fact that she chose to deal with the crooked detective, and he tried to talk her out of it several times, but she wouldn't listen. He just hoped it didn't come back and bite both of them in the ass.

"Why you change the location?" Bo asked, glancing back at the road in front of him. Tawana looked in the front seat mischievously.

"I'm about to bake the biggest cake you've ever seen," Tawana answered wickedly with a laugh that sent chills down Bo's spine. He knew from seeing Tawana's work firsthand what she was capable of and hated it for Detective Bass.

The next few miles was made in silence until Tawana made another call. "Ant, meet me at The Queen's Palace," she instructed. "Yeah, now!" she barked, and then ended the call and handed Bo his phone back.

~ ~ ~

"Who was that?" Chelsea asked when Ant jumped out of bed and began putting on his clothes. Ant knew she was upset, by the tone of her voice. He had promised her a day filled with sex and cuddling, up until he stepped out later on that night to do his pick-ups.

"I got to go meet up with B.B.," he explained, strapping up the laces to his boots.

"How long will you be gone?" Ant could hear her moving on the bed behind him.

"I don't got time for this shit right now," he said to himself and then turned around. He was just about to tell her to chill with all of her questions, until he spotted her lying in the middle of his bed with her legs spread wide open, playing in her wetness.

"Well, don't be too long. You wouldn't want to keep her waiting, would you?" she asked seductively. Before he could give her an answer, Chelsea removed her fingers from her opening and put them in her mouth.

"It won't be long," he promised, adjusting his erection. He wanted to jump back in bed to get a quickie, but knowing business needed to be handled, he grabbed his gun and keys off of the nightstand and headed for the door.

~ ~ ~

Tawana and Ant sat patiently in her office at The

Queen's Palace looking at the monitor on the wall as she ran down her plan for Detective Bass. "Here he comes now." They both watched as he pulled his car between Tawana's Bentley truck and Ant's Range Rover. As soon as Bass stepped out and placed his cell phone in his pocket, he headed to the front door of the club and hit the buzzer. "It's open," Tawana spoke through the intercom beside the door scaring Bass half to death.

Bass walked into the spacious strip club and looked around. It seemed much larger than the last time he was there. When he looked past the bar area, he noticed Tawana walking down a set of stairs. "Come," she motioned, making a left when she hit the bottom. Bass smiled when he noticed her making her way to the elite VIP section of the club. He had heard wild rumors of the things that went down on the other side of those doors and couldn't wait to see if any of them were true. If they were, he was about to have the time of his life.

Bass's eyes were on Tawana's ass the entire time. When they made it to the back, he noticed something was off. "So, where's your big bodyguard?" he asked as Tawana opened a door and led Bass to one of the exclusive rooms in the elite section.

"Who, Bo? I sent him off. He's chilling," she answered as she made her way over to the bar area to fix them a drink. Bass gawked at how her dress inched in and out of the crack of her ass and wondered how it would feel to take its place. Tawana returned with a glass of champagne for her and a cranberry juice for him. She had learned on their couple of dates he didn't indulge in alcohol.

"So, why the change of location?" Bass asked. He was hoping she wanted the same thing he did.

"We're both grown, right?" she responded, taking the seat next to Bass on the plush sectional.

"Of course," he answered, running his finger through his tie to loosen it up. All of a sudden, it began to get warm. Bass quickly downed the entire glass in one gulp.

"Good." Tawana licked her lips, leaned in close, and then placed her hand on his inner thigh. Bass closed his eyes tightly when she ran her tongue around the inside of his ear. Bass was in Heaven. He didn't know if he was high off knowing he was about to smash the sexiest woman he ever laid eyes on or if she had slipped something into his drink. It all came clear to him when the door to the room flew open and Tawana stood to her feet.

"What did you put in my drink?" he asked, looking up at Tawana. Her mouth was moving, but due to the effect of the drugs she had put in his drink, he was unable to comprehend. He tried to keep his eyes open as long as he could, until it was useless and then he blacked out.

~ ~ ~

"Nice of you to join us," Tawana spoke once she noticed Bass's movement. Bass looked from left to right trying to figure out where the voice was coming from. Better yet, where he was at. He knew he was in some type of freezer due to the chill coming from the vents mounted high on the walls. What he couldn't quite figure out was why he was butt naked tied to a chair. He heard footsteps nearing until Tawana finally came into view. She no longer had the look of an angel like she had earlier. Now she looked like a woman ready to go to war. Tawana slid the hood from over her head and looked down at the detective. "We can do this the easy way—" she smiled "—or we can do it the hard way." Ant slowly walked into view with a P-90 pistol gripped in his hand.

"Do you know who the fuck I am?" Bass questioned. Instead of getting a response, he received a smack in his face by Ant with his pistol. After shaking the dizziness off, Bass looked up at Ant and smiled. "YOU'RE DEAD; YOU SON OF A BITCH," he shouted before spitting out a mouth full of blood.

"Look, Bass, all I need to know is who the rat in the crew is?" Tawana explained. Bass smiled through bloodied lips before responding.

"You're gonna rot in prison, you fucking bitch. I got all I need to put you and that nigger Tamar in prison for the rest of y'all's miserable lives," he promised. "King slipped away, but you won't, B.B." Tawana was taken back by Bass's last statement. Not that she was going to rot in prison for the rest of her life, but him mentioning King's name, not to mention him calling her by her street name. No one in New Jersey had actually seen B.B. before. She was a ghost to everyone except her immediate family.

"Your time is up, Bass." She smiled. He didn't know it, but his statement confirmed what Jay had relayed to her earlier. "You and your snitch will rest in hell together." Tawana walked up to Bass and turned his head in the direction of the far corner.

"Wait! Wait! Wait!," he pleaded as he looked at his informant Bo with his throat slit from ear to ear with his tongue hanging from it. "That's what she meant when she said Bo was chilling." Bass looked up, and in one swift motion, B.B. gave his head a quick twist, and just like that, Bass was gone.

"What's so funny?" Tawana asked when she turned to the laughing Ant.

"I always heard you deserved it when you died with your eyes open," he replied, looking Bass in his lifeless eyes.

"I guess you're right," B.B. agreed. After giving Ant the instructions to get rid of the bodies, Tawana headed home to spend time with the love of her life. "Everything is taken care of," she relayed to the caller on the other end of the phone.

"Good! Good! We'll be flying back first thing in the morning," Jay replied. That was like music to Tawana's ears. Today couldn't have gone any better. She had killed two birds with one stone. Jay's news was the topping on the cake.

~ ~ ~

After Ant got rid of the two bodies, he headed home to finish up his day with Chelsea. He thought about how his life had made a drastic change from when he was back home in North Carolina, and he owed it all to B.B. No sooner than he pulled up to his condo, Ant's cell phone vibrated. It was a text from B.B. that read, *"You have just been promoted."*

"YES!" Ant screamed as he put the car in park. Once he killed the engine, he headed into the condo to give Chelsea the good news.

"Oh my God! That's great, Anthony!"

"That's what I said." Ant removed his clothes and jumped into bed, ready to get his groove on. Chelsea rode him for an hour straight before he flipped her over and pounded her out for another thirty minutes. When it was all said and done, Ant ended it by exploding down her throat. Exhausted, Ant lay on his back staring up at the ceiling with a smile on his face.

"When we finish making the pick-ups for tonight, you gonna take me shopping?" Chelsea asked as she cuddled up beside him. Ant looked over at her with wrinkles covering his forehead before answering.

"What kind of fucking question is that?" he asked. Chelsea lowered her head and rested it on his chest. "Of course, I am." Chelsea raised her head quickly.

"You need to stop playing all the time, boy." She smiled and then playfully hit Ant on his chest.

"Come on. Let's finish up in the Jacuzzi," he suggested, and Chelsea happily agreed. They both jumped out of bed and ran to the bathroom. They had another round of dirty sex until it was time to handle their business, and just as promised, when they finished, Ant took Chelsea on an all-out shopping spree.

"I'm so glad I met you," he told her on the way back home.

"I'm glad I met you too," she replied, looking at the $4K diamond ring he had just purchased for her. "Damn!" she cursed. Not only was he making it hard for her to do what she had to do, but he was also actually making her fall in love with him. "This is gonna be harder than I thought," she said to herself and then closed her eyes and leaned her seat all the way back and prepared herself for the drama that lay ahead in the future.

11

For the past few weeks, Hadji had stayed by Sherry's side day and night. The times he didn't were when she went over to Mia's place to get a breath of fresh air and peace of mind. Hadji took that time to get his plan together and work himself back into shape. "You sure you're ready to jump back into action?" Malek asked him as he spotted Hadji.

"As ready as I'm gonna be," Hadji answered, pushing the 275-pound weight up off his chest.

"Come on, bruh. You can do it," Maleki coached as Hadji struggled with the weight. Hadji closed his eyes and gave it one last push to get it off of him. "That's what I'm talking about," Maleki smiled as he reached down to pull Hadji up off the weight bench. Once Hadji was on his feet, Maleki lay down on it.

"Show off," Hadji declaimed as Maleki did the reps with ease. As Maleki continued his workout, Hadji and Malek walked over to the refrigerator and got them a fresh bottle of water.

"So, when are you leaving?" Malek asked.

"First thing in the morning," Hadji answered. Malek placed his bottle on the nearby table and looked at his friend with concern.

"So soon?"

Hadji knew it may have been too soon to head out on his mission, but he didn't want to delay it any longer. His cousin Sean had been dead for too long to let Ant continue breathing. Besides, he didn't know when or if the opportunity would fall so sweetly into his lap the way it had now. He didn't believe in coincidence. "I got this, homie," he assured Malek.

"What you two weaklings over here talking about?" Maleki asked when he made his way over, breaking the awkward moment of silence that fell on the two friends.

"Nothing," Hadji played it off. "Malek here was just telling me how he broke you down the last time you two worked out together," Hadji answered, placing his hand on Malek's shoulder. Malek put on a fake smile and played along with Hadji.

"Man. That nigga fronting! He came in at the end of my workout and tried to show off," Maleki claimed. Even though it was true, Maleki knew that though he was more muscular than Malek, Malek was much stronger, not to mention he had more book smarts. Where Maleki stood strong was in the art of war. They all shared a hearty laugh until Hadji announced he had to get back to Knightdale.

While Malek headed back into their mansion, Maleki walked Hadji to his car. "You know you can't fool me," Maleki said once Hadji let down his window. Before Hadji could respond, Maleki continued, "You want me to take the trip with you, bruh?" he asked his friend. Hadji looked up into his eyes and saw the sincerity.

"Thanks, bruh, but I got this," he assured him. "Besides, you got a wife and kids to take care of." Maleki knew trying to talk Hadji into letting him ride shotgun with him was useless, so he gave him a salute and stepped back from the car. "I'll call you when I get back," Hadji called out as he drove off the grounds.

~ ~ ~

As soon as Hadji walked into his home, he was greeted by the aroma of fried chicken in the air. After hanging his jacket on the rack beside the front door, he kicked off his shoes and headed to the kitchen where

Sherry was preparing dinner. Hadji stood in the doorway for a few seconds and admired his wife's beauty before announcing his presence. "You sure got it smelling good up in here," he admitted. Startled, Sherry dropped the piece of fried chicken she was turning over back into the grease, making a couple of specks splash on her arm.

"SHIT!" she cursed and looked at her forearm.

"You okay?" Hadji asked as he rushed over to assist her. After removing the fork from the chicken, Hadji grabbed Sherry's hand and looked down at her arm.

"I'm okay, babe. You just frightened me a little, that's all." Hadji lifted his head and looked into her eyes.

"I'm sorry, babe."

"It's okay." Sherry removed her hand from his and continued to fry the chicken. "Dinner will be ready shortly," she said over her shoulder. Hadji knew she was letting him know she didn't need him over her while she cooked. He put on a smile and headed toward the exit. Before he made it out, Sherry called his name.

"Yes, babe?" he turned and answered. With a smile on her face, she looked in her husband's eyes then told him.

"I love you."

"I love you more," he replied without a shadow of a doubt in his own tone. After catching the kiss she blew to him, Hadji caught it and placed it to his heart. Hadji turned and headed upstairs, taking the stairs two at a time until he reached the top. To his surprise, when he stepped inside his bedroom, a set of clothes were laid out for him.

~ ~ ~

After the nice candle-lit dinner Sherry prepared for them, they retreated to their bedroom for some quality time together. Something they had not had in a long time. "Do you remember when we first started dating and we used to eat dinner and then watch movies every Sunday after you came home from church?" Hadji asked, reflecting back to when he first pursued her. Sherry took her eyes off of the television set and looked over at him.

"Of course, I do," she admitted. She had the same angelic look she had the day he met her. "You thought you were going to get you some then, didn't you?" she teased, and then pinched his arm.

"You know you wanted it," he accused, pulling his arm away.

"If I did, I would have gave it to you."

"Well, what about now?" Hadji challenged with his hand moving around under the covers until he found what he was looking for.

"What are you doing?" Sherry whispered, trying to slow her breathing.

"What? You want me to stop?" Hadji asked, concerned. He had no idea if it was too early for them to have sex or not and did not want to chance the possibility of something going wrong.

"No, don't stop." It had been a while since they had been together sexually, and she longed to feel him inside of her. Hadji played in her wetness until he got her nice and wet. "Oh, babe," she whispered with her eyes closed as Hadji licked his way down south. Hadji could barely hear her cry out his name through all of the slurping and sucking sounds that vibrated throughout the room. He knew she was on the verge of cumming. She grabbed the sides of his head and began to rotate her hips like a belly dancer until she exploded all over his face. "HADJI!" she screamed out and pushed his head. It was to no avail. Hadji worked his tongue until Sherry was to spun and weak to resist any longer. When Hadji rose from up under the covers, Sherry looked at him lustfully.

"Now it's my turn." Before Hadji got a chance to say a word, she mounted him, reverse cowgirl style, and went to work.

"DAMN!" he shouted as she slammed and bounced her rear on his midsection. Sherry was releasing all of the pent-up frustration she had been holding in for the past month. They went at it for two hours straight before Sherry let up. When they were done, Hadji lay in bed staring up at the ceiling, trying to figure out a way to tell Sherry he needed to go out of town to handle some business. "Babe," he called out to her softly.

"I know," she responded, reading his mind. "Just promise me two things."

"And what's that?" he asked.

"Promise to come back to me in once piece?" she asked looking into his eyes.

"I can do that. What else?"

"Promise me you'll kill whoever did this to us?" Sherry's last request threw Hadji for a loop. Hadji knew he had to return as soon as possible because he was really worried about Sherry. A week after she came home from the hospital, she insisted she did not shoot him or try to take her own life, and that really bothered him.

"I promise," he told her and then held her tight in his arms. "I promise," he repeated, kissing the tear away from her cheek. Hadji closed his eyes and tried to prepare himself for what lay ahead of him. He just hoped he could keep his promise this time.

~ ~ ~

Hadji was up and dressed first thing in the morning. "If anything goes wrong, call me," he instructed Jamontae and Diontae as he loaded the last suitcase into the back of his Lexus.

"You know we got you," Diontae assured him.

"Uncle Hadji," Lil Sean screamed as he ran out the front door and raced toward his hero.

"What's up, Lil Sean?" Hadji smiled as he caught him in midair.

"Stop," Lil Sean giggled when Hadji began to tickle him.

"Nope," Hadji declined.

"Stop, Hadji, before you make him pee on himself,"

Mya shouted from the doorway with Sherry by her side. Hadji released Lil Sean, but not before giving him one last tickle for the road. When Lil Sean got to his feet, he took off like a bat out of hell back to his mother and then licked his tongue out at Hadji. Hadji made his way up the steps, never taking his eyes off of his wife. Even with a scarf wrapped around her head, she looked amazing.

"I'll call you as soon as my plane lands," he assured her and then leaned in and pressed his lips against hers.

"EWE!" Lil Sean frowned from his hiding spot behind Mya's leg.

"I got to get going." Hadji gave her one last kiss and then made his way back down the steps. "Take care of my wife," he told Jamontae and Diontae when he walked up to them.

"With our lives," Diontae promised. When Hadji looked over and saw Jamontae nodding his head in agreement, he knew Sherry's life was in good hands. After bidding his family farewell, he got in his car and headed to Slim's place to meet Fuzzy for their flight.

After driving nearly five minutes down the winding roads, Hadji pulled his car in front of Slim's mini castle.

The place brought back so many memories of his late mentor, Mr. Biggs. He thought about the mission that lay ahead of him as he killed the engine. It had been a few years since his cousin Sean had been killed. That was a few years too long, and his killer was still breathing. Hopefully, in the next twenty-four hours, he would be able to sleep peacefully at night. "Good, she's already here," Hadji thought to himself when he noticed Fuzzy's Maybach parked a few cars up. Even though he was glad she was on time, he dreaded seeing her. He planned to get the full details of what happened between them the night before he got shot.

"Hadji," Slim greeted him once he stepped onto the back patio.

"Slim," Hadji walked up and gave Slim a firm handshake, a quick embrace, and a pat on the back. Once he took a step back, Hadji acknowledged Fuzzy.

"The jet is fueled up and ready," Slim announced, placing a hand on Hadji's shoulder and guiding him off the patio to the awaiting car that sat at the edge of the backyard. Fuzzy followed a few feet behind to give them some privacy as they talked about future plans for the family business.

The ride down the private road that led to the airstrip was short, and after everything was loaded, they said their goodbyes. Right before Fuzzy boarded the jet, Slim leaned down and whispered in her ear, "I advise you to tell him as soon as possible," he warned.

"I will," she promised, knowing he was right. She knew she couldn't keep her secret from him much longer. After a long embrace, Fuzzy gave Slim an assuring smile and then boarded the jet. Hadji lay stretched out on the couch with one leg hanging off and his forearm over his eyes. Fuzzy made her way over to the plush leather recliner across from him and stared out the window. Slim was waving them off as the plane began to gather speed down the runway. Within seconds, the mini castle disappeared in the distance. After taking one more look over at Hadji resting peacefully, Fuzzy closed her eyes and did the same.

~ ~ ~

About a mile before Hadji and Fuzzy reached their destination, they spotted it. At first, Hadji thought it was an actual airport because the estate was so large. They both looked on in amazement as the jet circled the town onto the runway.

"Welcome," Ann greeted as the two descended the steps of the jet.

"Aunt Ann." Fuzzy smiled and took off full speed into her aunt's warm and motherly embrace.

Ann was the older sister of Mr. Biggs and Slim. She introduced Mr. Biggs into the game and groomed him into the kingpin he became shortly after their mother died. A few years later, Ann relocated to New Jersey, got married, and set up shop with her husband. She rode the high horse until he was killed one night over a card game. That's when she decided to retire.

"How was the flight?" Ann asked, looking from one to the other. Slim had told her about the thing Fuzzy had for Hadji.

"It was fine," Fuzzy answered as Hadji checked out his surroundings. He had been on a lot of grounds, but Ann's place was by far the largest. He remembered his mentor, Mr. Biggs, mentioning his sister and how she had taught him everything he knew. Now he was a firm believer after seeing her with his eyes. She looked wise beyond her years.

"Come," Ann instructed and then led the way to the awaiting stretch Navigator. After everything was loaded, the driver hopped in and drove them back to her place.

Ann's place was nothing like Hadji or Fuzzy had ever seen before. At least not on this side of the continent. The sky-high stone walls that surrounded it gave it a gothic look. "This is beautiful," Fuzzy admitted as the iron gates slid apart and the driver drove through the vineyard. Hadji was like a kid in a candy store, taking in all of the scenery. What caught his eye the most were the variety of ATVs and tracks that sat off in the distance. He made a mental note to take one of them for a spin before they headed back to North Carolina. "You might can learn a thing or two," Fuzzy leaned over and whispered to Hadji teasingly. Hadji looked over at her with arched brows and sucked his teeth. "Don't let this pretty face fool you," she responded. She then looked out the window. "And fat ass," she added, looking over her shoulder and down at her rear, catching Hadji doing the same. Seconds later, the door opened and the driver was escorting Ann out of the truck. Out of nowhere, Hadji's door opened, catching him off guard, and he found himself reaching for the gun he had in his waistline. "Come on," Fuzzy instructed, placing her hand over his to relax him.

"Come on you two lovebirds," Ann teased from the top step. Hadji shook the chill that came over him and slid his hand from under hers and then stepped out of the truck. By the time he made it to the other side of the SUV, Fuzzy was making her way up the steps.

"This is amazing," he could hear Fuzzy say as Ann led her into the fortress. She was right. The hallway was long and wide with chandeliers hanging from the fifty-foot ceiling along the way. Hadji was so lost in his thoughts as he walked, he didn't realize he had passed the doorway Ann and Fuzzy had ducked off into, until he heard his name being called.

"Hadji. We're in here." Hadji turned around and entered the doorway the laughter was coming from. When he walked into the kitchen, there were several cooks going about their daily routine with chef hats adorning their heads while Ann and Fuzzy sat side by side at a long table. It resembled the table Nino Brown sat at when he called the meetings on the movie, New Jack City. Hadji felt like a king as he made his way over to the head of the table to take a seat.

"Hadji, come sit next to me." Fuzzy waved him over before he could pull the chair back. He was about to decline, but the look she gave him let him know it was not up for debate.

"Excuse me for a second, chile." Ann stood to her feet and then made her way over to one of the chefs and whispered in his ear.

"Relax, Hadji. I just told you to come sit beside me because you were about to sit in my uncle's favorite chair," she explained. Hadji looked down the table at the empty seat and understood.

"I hope you two like fried chicken, mashed potatoes, string beans, corn, biscuits, and peach cobbler," Ann ran down the list of foods each chef had in their trays in front of them. "I know. I know. What black family from the South don't?" They all laughed as the food was set on the table and plates were prepared.

After filling their stomachs, Ann led the way to the west wing where Hadji and Fuzzy would be sleeping. "I hope you like it." Ann opened the door to the room Hadji would be sleeping in first and then stepped to the side to get his approval. Hadji couldn't believe his eyes. The bedroom was damn near the size of his master bedroom and the two adjoining rooms beside it at his place. "This is fine," he admitted as he walked in to get a better view. To his surprise, when he walked into the closet, his suitcases were neatly stacked on the back wall.

"If you need anything, just hit the number two on the phone and the butler will be here within seconds," Ann instructed, turning on her heels. "You are not a guest here," she told Fuzzy and then pointed to the far side room. "Your room is through that door." Hadji and Fuzzy looked at the door and then at one another.

"This is going to be a long stay," Hadji said to himself as he watched the fire dance in Fuzzy's eyes.

"Well, this old lady is about to get some much-needed rest," Ann yawned before stretching her arms. "If y'all need anything just give me a holla," Ann shouted over her shoulder. She then threw up the peace sign.

"That lady is something else," Fuzzy laughed as she made her way over to the nightstand and grabbed the remote from the top of it. Hadji watched her make herself comfortable and then begin to channel surf.

"I'm about to go take a shower," he told her after walking deep into the closet to retrieve his things. He knew he had to get away from her before he ended up doing some things he knew he would regret. It still ate at him, not knowing if they actually had sex the night he stayed over at her place. As soon as he finished what he came to Jersey for, Hadji was going to get the much-needed answers that haunted his thoughts day in and day out.

When Hadji made it out of the shower, Fuzzy was laid out across his bed, asleep. He stood at the doorway with a towel wrapped around the lower half of his body. He had to admit, she was definitely a sight to see. So many thoughts ran through his mind, but there was one that stood out the most. SHERRY! With that, Hadji walked over to Fuzzy, took the blanket, sat at the foot of the bed, and gently placed it on top of her. "Mmmmm," Fuzzy moaned. Then her eyes fluttered open. "You take longer than a woman," she joked. She then sat up in the middle of the bed. The sound of her voice and the glow on her face stirred up a feeling deep inside of him, and from the bulge in Hadji's mid area, Fuzzy knew it.

"What are you doing?" Hadji asked as Fuzzy slid to the foot of the bed and stood up in front of him. Instead of answering him, Fuzzy looked Hadji up and down.

"I'm sorry," Fuzzy whispered, running her fingers over the two bullet hole scars on his chest. Hadji grabbed her hands.

"They weren't your fault," he assured her with a smile. Fuzzy closed her eyes from his touch. Hadji knew she blamed herself for what happened that morning at her place.

"Hadji, we need to talk," Fuzzy told him after opening her eyes, remembering the promise she made Slim before boarding the jet. She figured now was a better time than ever to reveal her secret.

"What's up?" he asked, figuring she was finally going to tell him what really happened with them that night. When she removed her hand from his and placed it over her stomach, Hadji felt like he was about to die. "She can't be pregnant," he said to himself. They were interrupted by a knock at the door. "Hold on. I'm coming." Fuzzy found herself smiling outwardly as Hadji ran his fingers around the top of his towel. "Turn around," he stopped and told her.

"Don't act like that." Fuzzy waved him off and continued to look. Once she realized he was serious, she looked away out of respect. Once Hadji changed into something more appropriate, he walked over and opened the door. When he did, he saw Ann standing there with a huge smile spread across her face.

"I hope I wasn't interrupting anything." She looked past Hadji and found Fuzzy standing at the foot of the bed with her arms folded over her chest.

"Not at all," Fuzzy assured her, bending down to pick up her heels. "I'm about to go take a shower and get some rest. I am exhausted." Fuzzy walked over to the door that led to her room and opened it.

"I bet you are," Ann mumbled and then giggled. Ignoring her aunt, Fuzzy turned to Hadji.

"What time are we heading out?" she asked.

"I'll let you know as soon as I get the call." After Hadji's response, Fuzzy walked through the threshold and closed the door behind her. Ann could clearly see the attraction between the two, but she also knew there was more to the story than what was being told to her. She just couldn't put her finger on it.

"Well, I just came to tell you me and Fuzzy will be going to meet some relatives later, and to let you know you are free to join us if you would like," Ann said, looking him in the eyes.

"I'll think about it and will let you know later. Right now, all I want to do is get some rest." Ann nodded in understanding and took a step back out the door.

"Fair enough. Now you get you some rest and I will see you later on in the evening." Hadji nodded as Ann turned and strolled down the hallway with no care in the world. Hadji closed the door and walked over to the bed with thoughts of his future running through his mind. He had planned to break the news of his retirement to Fuzzy and the crew after he returned to North Carolina. He knew they would take it hard, but he explained in the beginning he was only in it for a short period, and once he killed Ant, his obligations would be over. He knew the hardest thing he would have to do is explain his departure to Diontae and Jamontae, because they had really grown on him in the past few months. They reminded him of himself and his late cousin Sean when they were young, hungry, and jumping off of the porch into the game. He'd face that road when the time came. Until then, he planned to get some rest.

~ ~ ~

Hadji was awaken by the buzzing of his cell phone. When he looked at the screen, he realized he had missed two previous text messages from Cee-Cee. All of them with the same address inside. They were five minutes after one another. After sliding on his all-black army fatigue suit, Hadji grabbed his duffle bag out of the closet. Once he made sure everything was intact, he headed over to Fuzzy's room. He stared in at her for a while before deciding not to wake her. He knew she would be mad at him for the choice he made to go alone, but he felt it was for her safety. Besides, the mission he was about to set out on was personal. Once he settled the score, he would help her get Junior back.

Hadji made it downstairs and found Ann siting in an oversized recliner with her feet kicked up. "I need to borrow a car," Hadji stated when he walked into the room. Instead of replying, Ann pointed to an end table with a set of car keys on it. "I'll be back later," he told her once he placed the keys in his coat pocket and headed back across the room to make his exit. Still Ann said nothing. It wasn't until Hadji made it down the hall and opened the front door that Ann said her first sentence.

"Don't bring the car back here." It was a simple request, but it was understood loud and clear.

"No doubt," Hadji shouted back at her and then closed the door behind him.

The blacked-out Lincoln LS was parked on the side of the garage next to the fortress. After getting in and adjusting the seat, Hadji put the address Cee-Cee sent him into the GPS system. "You will reach your destination in 12.3 miles," it announced automatically. On the ride to his destination, all Hadji could do was think about his cousin.

"This is for you, Cuzo," he promised looking up at the sky through the sunroof.

12

Ant pulled his Range Rover up in the parking space in front of his condo after taking Chelsea out to dinner. "Did you enjoy yourself?" he asked as they made their way up to the front door.

"I enjoy myself every time we are together," she flirted. She then looked back over her shoulder at her man. "What are you looking at?" she asked, already knowing the answer.

"That!" Ant took the back of his hand and smacked Chelsea on her ass and then watched it jiggle.

"Ouch, boy!" Chelsea hurried to get her house key out of her handbag before Ant decided to smack her on the ass again. The first thing Chelsea did when she opened the door was head straight for the bathroom. She had been holding her urine in ever since they left the restaurant. There was no way she was going to use a public restroom, even if it was inside of a five-star restaurant.

"I thought you said you paid the light bill the other day," Ant shouted down the hall when he hit the light switch and the light didn't turn on.

"I did," she claimed. Ant was about to say something else, until he spotted a shadow moving quickly his way through the darkness. "Oh shit," was his last words before everything turned black.

When Ant came to, he was bound to a chair in the middle of a dimly lit cold basement. He looked around the room and tried to figure out where he was at. He knew it wasn't his place because his condo didn't have a basement. "Tsk. Tsk. Tsk. You didn't think you could hide forever," Ant heard a voice call out from the dark corner to his left. He squinted his eyes trying to make out who the voice was coming from. Due to it being muffled from the ski mask covering the individual's face, it was hard for him to identify him or her.

"Chelsea," he whispered. "If you touched one hair on my fiancé's head, I'ma kill you," he threatened, trying to break free from the straps around his wrist.

"Cee-Cee is the least of your worries right about now," Hadji promised, taking a step closer. A chill ran down Ant's spine when the man removed the mask from his face.

"Hadji," Ant said in disbelief. "How did you know where—" Ant began to say. Then he thought back to all of the signs Chelsea gave him. That's when it hit him. Chelsea went back to key in the code for the alarm to the condo, but instead of arming it, she disarmed it and told

Hadji they were leaving.

"Hadji. I found the safe," Cee-Cee said as she made her way down the steps of the basement.

"YOU FUCKING BITCH," Ant cursed then bit down on his bottom lip.

"Is that the way you talk to your future wife?" Hadji asked, and then drew back and punched Ant in his mouth. The echo in the basement was so loud it made Cee-Cee jump.

"We need the combination," she whispered to Hadji, never taking her eyes off of Ant. Hadji took off his coat and then handed it over to Cee-Cee.

"We can do this the easy way or we can do this the hard way," Hadji explained while cracking his knuckles. Ant thought long and hard before giving his answer.

"Fuck you, nigga! When B.B. find out you here, she gonna have your stupid ass marked," Ant laughed before adding, "just like I marked your bitch-ass cousin Sean." Hadji punched Ant in his stomach, making him throw up the food he had just eaten. No matter what Hadji did, Ant wasn't breaking.

"Step back, Hadji," Cee-Cee demanded. Hadji took a step to the side and looked over in her direction. Ant looked through swollen eyes as Chelsea walked over to him.

"What the fuck you gonna do, bitch?" he laughed and

then spit a mouth full of blood on her heels. Before he could get another word out, Cee-Cee spit a razor out of her mouth and went to work.

"This what I'ma do, nigga," she said between slices. "Who's the bitch now?" she asked as Ant screamed and wiggled.

"OKAY! OKAY!" Ant shouted. "I'll give it to you." Hadji grabbed Cee-Cee's wrist right before she got the chance to run her razor across his throat. Out of breath, Cee-Cee stuck her tongue out and licked the blood off of it. Hadji was shocked, to say the least.

"What is it?" Hadji asked. After telling the code to the safe, Hadji ordered Cee-Cee back to the safe to see if it was correct. Once she was out of sight, Hadji looked down at her handiwork. Seconds later she was making her way back down the stairs. The smile on her face said it all. "Good job," Hadji said, pleased. "Do you have any last request?" he asked Ant before loading a round into the chamber.

Ant thought long and hard before answering. "Tell my son I love him." Hadji thought about his cousin and the son he had to leave behind because of Ant.

"Fuck you and your son!" he laughed before sending four slugs into the center of his chest.

"Grab something to put the money in," Cee-Cee said before turning around and heading back up to the room the safe was in. Hadji looked around the basement until he ran across a Gucci duffle bag.

After they finished loading all of the money and wiping down everything they had touched, they headed toward the back door. "So what we gonna do about Ant's truck?" Cee-Cee asked.

"Nothing. Leave it out front." Cee-Cee hunched her shoulders and followed Hadji to the Lincoln parked out back.

"Look," Cee-Cee pointed when they pulled up to the corner.

"That's the detective's partner they killed the other day." Hadji looked at the detective sitting in an unmarked car a few houses down from the stash house. He wondered if he saw Cee-Cee drive up in the truck. Then again, it didn't matter because knowing her, after they split the money, she would be moving to another state. Hadji made a left, and a few minutes later, he was on Route 1, headed to the cheap motel he had rented earlier to divide things up.

13

Two days had passed and Detective Green still had not heard from his partner. He even stopped by his place, where Bass's wife informed him that Bass had not been home in two days. The last time he heard anything from Bass was through the text he sent when he was about to meet with Tawana. The text was simple and contained three letters and three numbers. That's what led Green to Ant's Range Rover, where he observed and then followed a young woman to the address on Brunswick Avenue. This was just a few houses down from the bar they had raided a few weeks back, where they had arrested Tamar. He was hoping she would lead him to the owner of the SUV.

Detective Green sat patiently for an hour before he decided to make his move. His plan was to knock on the door the young lady went into and ask her to speak with the owner of the vehicle parked out front. He was just about to reach for the door, when he looked up and spotted Tawana's Bentley truck park across the street.

"Where's her driver?" Green asked himself, remembering his partner mention that she never went anywhere without him. Green slid down in the comfort of his front seat and watched Tawana cross the street. "This can't be a coincidence," he thought. He was going to get to the bottom of what happened to his partner and best friend, one way or another. Instead of calling for backup, Green loaded a round into the chamber of his P-90 Ruger and then made his way to the front door of the two-story row house.

~ ~ ~

"Ant," Tawana called out as she entered the stash house. She had a nagging feeling in her gut something was wrong. She had been calling Ant for the past hour, but he wasn't answering. She even sent him a text telling him to hit back ASAP, and still she got no response.

Tawana walked through the house, commando style, until she reached the back room that contained the safe. "I knew it," she said to herself when she found it open. The fact that it had been broken into gave her the feeling Ant had gotten up enough balls to rob her. That was something she couldn't live with. Tawana put away her gun and dialed a number. On the second ring, the caller picked up. "If you see Ant, body that nigga," Tawana ordered.

"Say no more," Ashley replied and then ended the call. Tawana placed her cell back in her handbag and headed back toward the front door. That's when the crack in the basement door caught her eye. After redrawing her gun, Tawana crept over to the door. She cautiously took one step at a time until she reached the bottom. That's when she saw Ant tied to a chair in the middle of the basement. "What happened?" she asked Ant, who was holding on for dear life. Ant tried to speak, but the holes in his chest were making it very difficult to do.

"H-a-a," he gasped. Tawana bent down a little closer to make out what Ant was trying to say. "Hadji is here," he repeated, this time a little clearer.

"How did he find us?" Tawana asked herself out loud.

"Chelsea."

Tawana looked down at Ant in disbelief.

"I knew you were a tender-dick nigga! I should've left your stupid ass down in North Carolina." Tawana stood straight up and aimed her pistol to the middle of Ant's head. She knew he would most likely bleed to death from the bullet wounds he was already suffering from, but she wanted him dead immediately. Right before she was able to pull back on the trigger, she was interrupted.

"FREEZE!" she heard a voice yell out. "DROP THE GUN!" an order came shortly after. Tawana looked over her shoulder and recognized Bass's partner standing at the bottom of the steps with his gun drawn. "DROP IT NOW!" he shouted.

"Officer. Someone broke into my house and tied my boyfriend up and shot him," Tawana lied, stepping to the side so Green could see Ant's bullet-ridden body.

"SHIT!" Green cursed and rushed across the room. "This is detective Green. I need an ambulance at 539 Brunswick Avenue," Green called in. Before Green could get another word out, Tawana sent a slug to the back of his head, knocking him onto Ant.

"Stupid-ass nigga!" she barked. Then she placed a bullet between Ant's eyes for good measure. On her way back up the basement stairs, Tawana made a call. "You can cancel the hit I put out on Ant. It's taken care of.

Yeah, I'm sure. Send the cleanup crew to the stash house to clean up some mess," she ordered and then ended the call. Tawana knew there was about to be a lot of blood shed on the streets of Trenton. She just hoped it wasn't her own.

~ ~ ~

Did you hear what the fuck I said?" Tawana yelled into the phone at her sister. Crystal heard Tawana, but her emotions were all over the place. Even though she would never admit it, she had feelings for Ant. Deep down, Jay was just temporary until she decided to give Ant his shot. Now it was all ruined.

"Yeah, I heard you," Crystal finally replied. "We're going to fly out to North Carolina to see Jay's brother, and then we'll be back in Trenton to handle the problem," Crystal assured her.

"Hold on," Tawana told her sister when her other line beeped. "That's Mrs. Deloris." Tawana clicked over. "Hello. Okay. See you in a few." After she ended her call with Mrs. Deloris, Tawana clicked back over.

"What did she want?" Crystal asked.

"All she said was she was on the way and had a

relative she wanted me to meet. Hold on." Tawana covered the phone and called Junior's name. A minute later, he stuck his head inside of her room.

"Yes, Mommy?"

No matter what type of mood Tawana was in, Junior always had a way of lifting her spirits.

"Aunt Crystal's on the phone."

"Tawana," Crystal shouted. "I'ma get you, bit—" she shouted, but it was too late.

"Auntieee," Junior cheered into the receiver.

"Hi, sweetheart."

"Thanks for the new game." Junior went on without giving Crystal a chance to get a single word in. He ended it with, "You still gonna take me to the amusement park?"

"That boy don't forget nothing," Crystal said to herself before promising to take him as soon as she returned to Jersey. "Yep, as soon as I get back," she promised.

"Okay. Love you. Bye." Junior tossed the phone back to Tawana and ran back to his room to finish his game. Jay had insisted on sending one of his workers out to get Junior a new game the day before, and she was glad he did.

"Well, hooker, I'll see you when you get back," Tawana announced ready to end the call. "I love you too, and give my brother-in-law my love," Tawana teased. To her surprise, Crystal had her on speaker phone and Jay heard her.

"Back at ya, Sis," Jay replied in his deep Spanish accent. Then the line went dead.

Tawana shook her head as she placed her cell phone on the charger and then made her way across the room and into the hallway. "I wanna play," she sang from Junior's doorway. Junior's face lit up as he lifted up the other remote control and handed it to her. Tawana wanted to get in as much fun time as she could because in the next day or so, she would be hitting the streets to finish what she had started.

14

Hadji sat in the middle of the cheap hotel he had rented before heading over to the address Cee-Cee had given him earlier. It was located on Route 1, a short distance from Ant's condo. He counted up the money from the take while Cee-Cee went into the bathroom to take a shower and get Ant's dried-up blood off of her. "So how much did we get?" Cee-Cee asked, walking out of the shower butt naked.

"Damn!" Hadji cursed when he looked up. "You made me miscount." Cee-Cee smiled outwardly, seeing she still had that kind of effect on Hadji after all of the years that had passed between them. Hadji took his eyes off of her and began to recount the money in front of him. Cee-Cee walked over to the bed where the neatly stacked piles of money were and began to fumble through them. "Those are ten thousand stacks," he informed her. By the look of the stacks she could tell it was at least a half a million on the bed in front of her. "You ain't gonna put no clothes on?" Hadji asked, not able to keep his eyes off of her erect nipples.

"That's a first," she said with raised brows. Any other

time, Hadji would have been all over Cee-Cee. "If you may have forgotten, my clothes are ruined," Cee-Cee stated, offended. Hadji looked to his right, picked up his jacket, and then threw it in her direction.

"Here. Put this on." Cee-Cee caught the jacket in midair and looked at it like it had some type of disease. After dropping it to the floor, Cee-Cee began to help him recount their earnings.

When they were done counting, she finalized, "$634,000." Usually, Cee-Cee would have been jumping for joy.

"Come on, Cee. Why you tripping? You know I'm a married man now," Hadji tried to rationalize with her and convince himself at the same time. By the look in Cee-Cee's eyes, he knew he was failing miserably. "Come on, Cee. Chill," he pleaded once she began to bite on her bottom lip.

"Come on what, Hadji? Why you bugging? I know the rules." That was true because as long as they had been messing around, she never got out of line and gave him his space when needed. "No strings attached, right?" she asked as she made her way over in front of him. Before Hadji could respond, Cee-Cee shoved him forcefully down onto the bed and mounted him. He could feel her wetness soaking through the crotch of his fatigues. Giving in to his inner demons, Hadji didn't resist her advances any longer. After freeing his manhood, Cee-Cee raised up and placed it in her opening. That's when his cell phone began to ring.

"I got to answer that," he said, gripping her hips before she got a chance to sit down on him. "Don't say a word," he warned in a stern tone. Instead of responding, Cee-Cee dismounted his lap and got down on her knees. "Yeah," he answered at the same time as she placed him in her mouth. "WHAT!" Hadji questioned, forcing himself to the back of her throat. If it wasn't for the fact that she had her tonsils removed years ago, she would have gagged. "I'll be there in a couple of hours," he assured the caller. He then disconnected the call. "Get up," he ordered, but Cee-Cee ignored his demand. "STOP!" he shouted, a little annoyed. Cee-Cee knew something had to be wrong if Hadji was giving up getting some good head.

"Is everything okay?" she asked, concerned when she lifted her head.

"Get your clothes on! I gotta go!" he responded and then stood to his feet. Cee-Cee watched as his semi-erect penis hung low.

"What a waste," she said to herself as she climbed off of her knees to retrieve her clothes from the floor in the corner of the room. By the time she was dressed, Hadji had packed up all of his things and was out the door.

On the way to drop Cee-Cee off to get her car from Ant's place, Hadji relayed what the caller said on his cell at the room. "Do you want me to go back to North Carolina with you?" she asked, concerned. He knew she meant well, but Hadji didn't want to get her involved any more than she already was. Before he could respond, Cee-Cee poured out her heart to him. "Hadji, you know I will die for you, right?" Hadji knew she had love for him, but never imagined it ran so deep.

"I know you would, but I won't let you do that," he replied, never taking his eyes off of the road. The rest of the ride was made in complete silence. When they arrived, Cee-Cee grabbed her things and got out of the car without saying goodbye. Hadji knew she was upset with the decision he made, but he couldn't let her ruin her life any further. Cee-Cee was a good girl, in her own type of way. Once she walked away from the car, she heard Hadji pulling out of the parking lot. She thought not to watch him drive away, but couldn't resist.

"What the—" When Cee-Cee turned around, she spotted a large bag where Hadji's car had sat.

When she went to see what it was, a tear trickled down her cheek. It was the other half of the money they had taken from Ant and B.B. Cee-Cee jumped when the cell phone on her hip began to buzz.

"This is good-bye," it read, followed by two hearts

holding hands.

"I love you too," she whispered before picking up the bag and walking back over to her car.

Once Hadji hopped back on Route 1, on the way back to Ann's, he called Fuzzy to let her know he received an important phone call and he would be leaving to go back home. "Okay, I will call you later on when we get back from visiting one of my relatives I have never met before," she said excitedly. "I never knew my family was so big."

"Okay. I will call you after I touch down in North Carolina and find out what's going on," he assured her.

"Hadji wait," she called out before he disconnected the call. She wanted to tell him the secret she had been holding in, but the words wouldn't come out. If Ann wasn't staring her in the face, it would have been a little easier.

"Hello," Hadji spoke into the phone.

"Hadji I—," Fuzzy began before she lost signal.

"HELLO! HELLO!" Hadji shouted into the phone. He had an idea of what Fuzzy was about to say, but wanted to be sure. Looking at the display screen that read, "Lost Call," Hadji sat the phone in his lap and thought about his future. "How would Sherry take the news if Fuzzy was pregnant?" was the first question that popped into his head. He shook the chills off of his body and then ran his fingers across the bullet wound that rested right above his heart. He knew the fate of his marriage depended on the predicament he had found himself in. Twenty minutes later, Hadji was pulling up to the awaiting jet that was ready to depart the estate.

15

When Ann pulled up to the front of their destination, Fuzzy had to admit she was quite impressed. It wasn't as big as the mansion she lived in with Speedy, but it wasn't far off. They got out of the SUV and walked up to the double doors. After fishing a set of keys out of her purse, Ann opened the door and led the way through the foyer. "We're here," Ann announced into the intercom.

"We'll be right down," they heard a feminine voice reply. Ann walked down the hallway with Fuzzy in tow, taking in all of the beautiful artwork lining the walls. She had to admit whoever lived in the mansion had a lot of taste. Expensive taste at that, because she had seen some of the same exact pieces at an art gallery many years ago. Halfway down the hall, one caught her eye. It was one of the universe, and under it, the caption read: "If this world was mine, I would give it to you."

"It can't be," she whispered, thinking of her ex-husband.

"Mommyyy," she heard a familiar voice call out, racing down the stairs in her direction. When Fuzzy turned around, she spotted Junior, followed by B.B., who was too busy on her phone to notice Fuzzy standing in the middle of the hall. It wasn't until she reached the bottom and looked up that she saw Junior in Fuzzy's arms. She hated the fact she had left her handbag upstairs with her gun in it.

"HELLO! HELLO!" the caller shouted into the phone, but Tawana didn't respond. Instead she pressed the End button.

"CLICK!"

"What are you doing here?" Tawana questioned, walking up to Fuzzy.

"I invited her," Mrs. Deloris interrupted.

"For what?" Tawana questioned Mrs. Deloris, clearly upset.

"Because this shit has been going on too long," she answered.

Tawana was taken back. Not by her answer, but because as long as she had known Mrs. Deloris, she had never cursed, not even once. "There is something you two need to know." They both waited patiently as Ann tried to find the words to say. "Tawana, do you know who your father is?" she asked. Tawana looked at Mrs. Deloris like she had lost her mind.

"What does that have to do with anything?"

"Just answer the damn question." Ann was getting irritated.

"His name was Wendell. Why?"

Mrs. Deloris smiled. "Wendell who?" she pressed.

"Wendell Williams," Fuzzy answered for her, figuring out why her Aunt Ann was asking her the question.

"How did you know that?" Tawana asked, confused.

"Because he is my daddy too," Fuzzy replied. The hallway seemed to get smaller to Tawana after realizing what they both were implying.

"That's right," Ann verified. After explaining that Slim promised King he would continue supplying him if he moved to New Jersey with Tawana and start a new life, things started to be a little clearer. "Too much blood would have been shed and Slim and I promised to raise you girls the best we could. We tried to keep y'all away from the street life, but as you two can see, that was impossible." Tawana and Fuzzy looked at one another and then back at Ann.

"So King knew you were my daddy's sister?" B.B. asked.

"Yes," Mrs. Deloris answered.

"So what is your real name, Deloris or Ann?"

"Both. My name is Deloris Ann Thompson, but you can call me Auntie now that everything is out in the open." She winked. Tawana felt all kinds of emotions. Hurt. Sadness. Betrayal. And most of all, jealousy. She was jealous because she felt like she had been cheated out of so many years of a father she only knew by the checks he sent her mother every month. Checks her mother called "hush money" to stay hidden from Fuzzy's mother, whom he was married to at the time before she died. Jealous she was cheated out of so many years she could have been spending with her older sister. Tawana remembered her mother telling her that her father gave her the name B.B. (Black Beauty). Her thoughts were interrupted by the sound of a ringing cell phone. Everyone looked at their screens.

16

The flight back to North Carolina only took forty-five minutes, but to Hadji it seemed like an eternity. "How was the flight?" Sheila asked Hadji, excited the jet headed in her direction. "That bad, huh?" she said after noticing the worried look on Hadji's face.

"You don't know the half," he replied as he walked over to the passenger's side of her car and then got in. Sheila hopped in the driver's seat and drove back to Slim's mini castle. Instead of talking, Sheila let Hadji think in peace.

"Where's Slim?" Hadji asked as they entered the large conference room in the basement.

"He should be here in about thirty minutes." She kept a close eye on the security monitor that watched Sade and Lil Menace in the theater room watching *Dora the Explorer*.

"So what was so important I needed to come back immediately?" Hadji asked. Even though he asked, he didn't think he was ready for the news that awaited him. Before Sheila got the chance to answer, his cell phone began to ring. "Hello. Okay. One," Hadji ended the call and then looked up at Sheila, who looked over at the monitor that overlooked the front entrance gate. Five minutes after she buzzed Diontae and Jamontae onto the grounds, they entered the basement.

"So what's so important we had to leave our post, boss?" Diontae asked. The brothers looked at Hadji, and Hadji looked at Sheila for the answer. Sheila touched the screen of one of the monitors. Then it went black. A few seconds later, the front of Fuzzy's mansion appeared on it. They watched silently as Sherry drove her car in front of the mansion and got out with a gun in her hand.

"What the—" Hadji mouthed when it registered to him it was the video of the day he got shot. She was only at the door for a couple of seconds before it opened and Hadji came into view. Hadji remembered everything like it was yesterday. Before they knew what happened, Hadji fell to the ground. "YO, REWIND THAT AGAIN," he shouted, standing to his feet. Hadji made his way over to the monitor without taking his eyes off the screen. Sheila played the scene over again, and it was plain to see Sherry didn't fire her gun once she raised it toward him. "So she didn't shoot me," he said out loud, but more to himself.

"Keep watching," Sheila instructed. They watched as Sherry's body tensed up as if she heard someone coming up behind her. When she tried to turn around and look,

197

BOOM!

"OH SHIT!" Diontae shouted when Sherry's head jerked to the side and her body went limp and landed beside Hadji's. Tears came to his eyes when a figure dressed in all black appeared. They all watched the figure hurry into Fuzzy's mansion and seconds later return with a CD disc in their hand. After the shooter traded guns with Sherry, they disappeared off of the screen again. They all were at a loss for words, until Slim entered the room smoking his signature Cuban cigar. Hadji's and Slim's eyes locked on one another's. "Don't even think about it," Sheila warned, pressing the small .380 she had in her hand to the side of Slim's head. Slim held his hands in the air. Diontae and Jamontae grabbed Slim by each arm and then set him in a chair.

"Hadji, when Fuzzy saw Sherry raise her gun, she lost it," Slim began to explain. "She wanted to tell you." Slim hunched his shoulders.

"TELL ME WHAT? HOW SHE SHOT ME AND SHERRY!" Hadji shouted.

"It was a mistake. Well, shooting you was a mistake. Maybe she was trying to get Sherry out of the way so she could have you to herself." Hadji placed his hand on his forehead and let out a deep sigh. "You knew the rules, Hadji. My brother taught you them." Slim looked at Hadji and smiled. "What was rule number one?" Slim asked him. Hadji thought back to the rules his mentor gave him.

"My daughter is off-limits," he repeated the first rule Mr. Biggs gave him. Slim inhaled a lung full of smoke and then exhaled it into the air.

"CALL HER!" Hadji demanded. Slim slowly retrieved his cell phone from his suit pocket and then dialed her number. When she got on the phone, he handed it to Hadji. Slim looked past the barrel pointed to the side of his head and stared into Sheila's eyes pleadingly. She was fighting not to pull back on the trigger as she reflected back to a time when she was happy, when she was alive, when she loved him.

Sheila was seventeen years old when Slim first pursued her. A small-time corner hustler for his older brother, Wendell, who later became the kingpin of the city, "Mr. Biggs." His suave and laid-back demeanor had all of the young girls chasing after him. She couldn't figure out why he always went after her since she wasn't the type of female to hang out with the cool kids or in the streets. It was no secret she was the prettiest girl in the neighborhood, and the most likely to succeed, and that alone made him want her more.

For an entire year straight, Slim was persistent, and it finally paid off. Sheila agreed to go out on a date with him. After that date, she found herself head over heels for

Slim. She also learned later that would be the biggest mistake of her life: giving her heart, body, and soul to a hustler.

Sheila was home cooking dinner for Slim when she received a telephone call informing her of her man's whereabouts. Before she knew it, she was storming out of the house and heading toward the newly purchased Toyota Slim had bought for her.

It only took a few minutes to get to the location, being that Slim hustled a few blocks away from their house. Sheila pulled up behind Slim's S-Class Benz and marched over, not knowing what to expect. Her heart broke in two when she spotted Slim on top of another woman, getting it in. Seeing Slim having unprotected sex with the neighborhood crackhead sent her over the edge. Slim looked up into Sheila's tear-filled eyes and tried to explain. "It's not what it looks like, baby," he promised. Sheila turned and ran to her car. Slim jumped out of the backseat with his pants to his ankles, running in her direction.

"I got something for his ass," Sheila said to herself as she started her car. If it wasn't for Slim tripping over his pant leg, Sheila would have run him over. Slim knew if he didn't hurry home, Sheila would be gone. To his surprise, when he pulled up to their house, it was burning to the ground. When Sheila left to go find him, she forgot to turn off the fried chicken.

Sheila found Slim a month later at the park he played ball in every weekend. She knew he would be there. Sheila pulled up behind his Benz and got out. "Ain't that your girl?" Mr. Biggs pointed. Slim looked up as Sheila placed a piece of paper under his windshield wiper blade. Biggs and every other ball player on the court laughed at Slim as he hurried over to try to catch up with Sheila before she got back in her car, but he was too slow. Slim snatched the paper off of his window and opened it. "Where you going, man? We got a game to finish," Biggs shouted as Slim jumped in his car, started the engine, and then raced off.

"Either finish the game or pay us our thousand dollars." Nelson grinned. Him and his partner were happy to see Slim leave, because they were losing. The score was five to nine. Mr. Biggs was heated. As long as him and Slim had been playing Nelson and his cousin Barry, they had never lost, and he knew if he lost now, he would never hear the end of it, even if it was by default.

"Ball in," Biggs said, checking the ball up at the top of the court. Nelson and Barry smiled at each other.

"Check," Nelson laughed. Three minutes and two shots later, Nelson and Barry were coming off of $500 apiece.

"Nice doing business with you two chumps," Biggs

laughed as he headed to his car, in search of his brother. When Biggs finally caught up with Slim, it was later on that night at the bar. "You owe me $500," Biggs teased, and then took a seat across the booth from him. Instead of verbally responding, Slim slid the piece of paper Sheila had left across the table. When Biggs read it, he looked up at his brother. "HIV," he mumbled. He had heard of it and the effects it had on people's lives, but he never knew anyone personally that had it. His heart went out to his brother. "Don't worry, bruh. We gonna get you cured," Biggs assured him. It didn't matter if it cost Biggs every dime he owned, he was going to try and save his brother's life. His heart also went out to Sheila. Before Biggs died, he promised to hold Sheila down, and he did.

When Sheila snapped out of her flashback, Slim was on the phone talking to someone. She watched as he conversed like he had no worries in the world. That's when she snapped. Sheila calmly walked over to Slim, raised her gun arm, and then pulled the trigger. Hadji, Diontae, and Jamontae all watched as Slim's body fell out of the chair he was sitting in. Slim's cell phone hit the floor at the same time and broke into a thousand little pieces. If Hadji wasn't quite ready for war, he surely was going to be now. Sheila looked down at Slim's body, her first love, and then hawked up a mouthful of phlegm and spat it on him before walking out of the room.

"Clean up this mess," Hadji ordered and then went after her. After giving her reason for ending Slim's life, Hadji understood. Hadji had always thought Sheila had contracted AIDS through sharing needles from tricking back when she was out in them streets. Never in a million years would he have imagined the reason she turned to drugs in the first place was to cope with having the deadly disease.

Thirty minutes later, the brothers entered the room.

"Y'all go on ahead and get up out of here. I'll take care of Murph and Forty," Sheila assured them. Hadji hugged Sheila and gave her a kiss on the cheek.

"If you need me for anything, just give me a call."

"I will." After another short embrace, Hadji, Diontae, and Jamontae headed out the door.

~ ~ ~

After reporting everything that had happened in Jersey to the twins, Hadji parked in his garage and sat for a minute, replaying the events of his life over the past few years. He had been through a lot during a short period of time. He had gotten married, shot, and arrested for murder, had killed people, and now he had to prepare for a war he was not quite sure he was ready for. He was snapped from his thoughts by Sherry tapping on his driver's-side window. "Is everything okay?" she asked when he opened the door to step out. He looked in his wife's beautiful face and thought about telling her it was, but he knew it wasn't.

"No," he answered honestly. He knew if he wanted to move the way he needed to keep them safe, he had to be completely honest with her. "Come on. Let's go inside and talk." Hadji held his hand out, and Sherry placed hers in his.

Hadji and Sherry sat in their bedroom where he told her everything that had happened. When he was done, Sherry had only one question that needed to be answered. "Did you have sex with her the night you stayed over at her house?" Hadji, not knowing the true answer, answered with the only answer he could.

"I don't know, babe. I can't remember." Sherry looked into her husband's eyes and deep into this soul and then placed her hand on his face.

"I believe you, Hadji," she promised him and leaned in and kissed his lips. Even though war was in the near future, Hadji was living in the here and now. He laid Sherry on their bed and began to undress her.

After they made love, Hadji lay on his back and watched Sherry sleep. "I love you," he whispered before closing his eyes to get some rest.

"I love you more," she replied with her eyes still closed.

Being kidnapped from her home, taking the life of a man that invaded their home and tried to kill her husband, and almost having her life taken by a woman that wanted her man turned Sherry's once kind and caring heart of gold into a sack of burning coal. She wanted nothing worse than getting revenge on Fuzzy, and that was what she planned to do if it took the last breath in her body to do it. Every time she looked in the mirror and saw the scar on her, she was reminded of that dreadful morning Fuzzy shot her in the head. "I'ma make you feel my pain if it's the last thing I do!" she promised before drifting off to sleep.

17

After getting the green light from Hadji and writing down the address, Maleki got dressed in all black and made his way downstairs to the garage. His eyes scanned the spacious room and the variety of vehicles, but he already knew which one he would be taking for his special mission. He walked over to his newly purchased Ducati and picked up the matching racing jacket that sat on the seat. Once it was securely wrapped around his frame, Maleki slid the helmet over his head. He hit the start button, and the bike came to life. Just hearing the exhaust gave Maleki a rush he couldn't explain. Maleki hopped on the mean machine and then hit the garage door opener. As soon as it was high enough to make an exit, he was bent over the gas tank and raced out of the garage. By the time he made it out of the driveway, Maleki had it on one wheel.

Thirty minutes later, Maleki had reached his destination. The entire ride over, all he could think about was putting a bullet in Fuzzy's head. He had told Hadji on more than one occasion he had a funny feeling she meant him no good, and usually his gut feelings never failed him.

Maleki parked his sport bike deep in the brush that outlined Fuzzy's place, out of the sight of any prying eyes. After he put in the security code Hadji had given him, Maleki boldly walked up the driveway to the front door. "This is too easy," he said to himself as he turned the gold handle on the front door and it slowly crept open.

After cautiously drawing his weapon and screwing the silencer to the tip of it, Maleki tip-toed into the foyer. "Not bad," he thought to himself, looking at the priceless painting that covered each side of the long hallway. The first room he entered was all white, down to the Persian rug. Even the countertop that covered the bar was white leather. Maleki decided to make himself a stiff drink while he waited on his victim to return home. He was on his second round of Scotch when he noticed a set of headlights pull up to the front of the mansion. Maleki made his way across the massive room and peered out of the window. When he spotted a set of legs step out from the drop head, Maleki raced for his position behind the front door entrance.

"Yeah, I'm here now." There was a short pause in her conversation before she continued. "Once I get the kids clothes together, I will be there." With her attention on the call, she never noticed Maleki in position to take her life. "How long will it take you to meet me?" she asked the caller on the other end. As she placed her foot on the first step, she noticed movement in the mirror on the wall. "NO, WAIT!" she shouted as Maleki raised his gun and then fired. One bullet hit the mirror, and the other went through the back of her head. Pst... Pst...

Maleki stepped out of the dark just as Lil Menace raced into the front door.

"Auntie," he called out, trying to catch his breath. "I gotta pee." He stood cemented in one spot when he spotted a figure lying at the other end of the hall on the stairwell. Maleki stood silently, trying to figure out his next move. He wanted to shoot Lil Menace in the back of his head and be done with it, but thought against it since he didn't see his face. Besides, he had big respect for his father. Lil Menace began to tremble when he noticed a shadow behind him. Before he knew it, urine was running down his leg. Lil Menace slowly began to turn in Maleki's direction.

"Shit," he cursed. Having no other option, he drew back and hit Lil Menace across his face with the butt of his gun, knocking him out instantly. Maleki turned and walked out of the mansion in a hurry. "What else can go wrong?" he thought as he made his way down the driveway. A strange feeling came over him, making him look over in the direction of Fuzzy's drop head. "Man, I'm tripping," he said to himself as he glanced over at the empty vehicle. After shaking the eerie feeling, Maleki proceeded down the driveway.

~ ~ ~

Sade waited until she heard the sound of a motorcycle racing down the street before she picked herself up from the floorboard of her mother's car. "MENACE!" she shouted after her cousin after jumping out of the car and running up to the mansion. After finding him on the floor in a puddle of blood, she walked on wobbly legs until she made it to him. "Wake up, Menace," she begged as she cradled his head in her lap. Her heart was breaking into a thousand pieces. First, she lost her father, then her brother, and now her cousin. She was snapped out of her trance by the sound of a cell phone ringing. She noticed a body at the end of the hall on the stairwell for the first time. Sade gently laid Menace's head to the floor and then stood to her feet. The closer she got to the body, she more slippery the floor became. She knew who the body belonged to before she reached it.

"HELLO. HELLO," the caller shouted when Sade connected the call. "What happened?"

Sade tried to tell the caller what had occurred, but only one word escaped her lips. "MOMMY!" she cried before passing out.

To order books, please fill out the order form below:
To order films please go to www.good2gofilms.com

Name: ___ _____

Address:_____

City: _____ State: _____ Zip Code: _____ _____

Phone:_____

Email:_____

Method of Payment: Check   VISA   MASTERCARD

Credit Card#:_ _____

Name as it appears on card: _____

Signature: _____

Item Name	Price	Qty	Amount
48 Hours to Die – Silk White	$14.99		
A Hustler's Dream - Ernest Morris	$14.99		
A Hustler's Dream 2 - Ernest Morris	$14.99		
A Thug's Devotion – J. L. Rose and J. M. McMillon	$14.99		
Black Reign – Ernest Morris	$14.99		
Bloody Mayhem Down South – Trayvon Jackson	$14.99		
Bloody Mayhem Down South 2 – Trayvon Jackson	$14.99		
Business Is Business – Silk White	$14.99		
Business Is Business 2 – Silk White	$14.99		
Business Is Business 3 – Silk White	$14.99		
Childhood Sweethearts – Jacob Spears	$14.99		
Childhood Sweethearts 2 – Jacob Spears	$14.99		
Childhood Sweethearts 3 - Jacob Spears	$14.99		
Childhood Sweethearts 4 - Jacob Spears	$14.99		
Connected To The Plug – Dwan Marquis Williams	$14.99		
Connected To The Plug 2 – Dwan Marquis Williams	$14.99		
Connected To The Plug 3 – Dwan Williams	$14.99		
Deadly Reunion – Ernest Morris	$14.99		
Dream's Life – Assa Raymond Baker	$14.99		
Flipping Numbers – Ernest Morris	$14.99		
Flipping Numbers 2 – Ernest Morris	$14.99		
He Loves Me, He Loves You Not - Mychea	$14.99		
He Loves Me, He Loves You Not 2 - Mychea	$14.99		
He Loves Me, He Loves You Not 3 - Mychea	$14.99		

He Loves Me, He Loves You Not 4 – Mychea	$14.99		
He Loves Me, He Loves You Not 5 – Mychea	$14.99		
Lord of My Land – Jay Morrison	$14.99		
Lost and Turned Out – Ernest Morris	$14.99		
Married To Da Streets – Silk White	$14.99		
M.E.R.C. - Make Every Rep Count Health and Fitness	$14.99		
Money Make Me Cum – Ernest Morris	$14.99		
My Besties – Asia Hill	$14.99		
My Besties 2 – Asia Hill	$14.99		
My Besties 3 – Asia Hill	$14.99		
My Besties 4 – Asia Hill	$14.99		
My Boyfriend's Wife - Mychea	$14.99		
My Boyfriend's Wife 2 – Mychea	$14.99		
My Brothers Envy – J. L. Rose	$14.99		
My Brothers Envy 2 – J. L. Rose	$14.99		
Naughty Housewives – Ernest Morris	$14.99		
Naughty Housewives 2 – Ernest Morris	$14.99		
Naughty Housewives 3 – Ernest Morris	$14.99		
Naughty Housewives 4 – Ernest Morris	$14.99		
Never Be The Same – Silk White	$14.99		
Shades of Revenge – Assa Raymond Baker	$14.99		
Slumped – Jason Brent	$14.99		
Someone's Gonna Get It – Mychea	$14.99		
Stranded – Silk White	$14.99		
Supreme & Justice – Ernest Morris	$14.99		
Supreme & Justice 2 – Ernest Morris	$14.99		
Supreme & Justice 3 – Ernest Morris	$14.99		
Tears of a Hustler - Silk White	$14.99		
Tears of a Hustler 2 - Silk White	$14.99		
Tears of a Hustler 3 - Silk White	$14.99		
Tears of a Hustler 4- Silk White	$14.99		

Tears of a Hustler 5 – Silk White	$14.99		
Tears of a Hustler 6 – Silk White	$14.99		
The Panty Ripper - Reality Way	$14.99		
The Panty Ripper 3 – Reality Way	$14.99		
The Solution – Jay Morrison	$14.99		
The Teflon Queen – Silk White	$14.99		
The Teflon Queen 2 – Silk White	$14.99		
The Teflon Queen 3 – Silk White	$14.99		
The Teflon Queen 4 – Silk White	$14.99		
The Teflon Queen 5 – Silk White	$14.99		
The Teflon Queen 6 - Silk White	$14.99		
The Vacation – Silk White	$14.99		
Tied To A Boss - J.L. Rose	$14.99		
Tied To A Boss 2 - J.L. Rose	$14.99		
Tied To A Boss 3 - J.L. Rose	$14.99		
Tied To A Boss 4 - J.L. Rose	$14.99		
Tied To A Boss 5 - J.L. Rose	$14.99		
Time Is Money - Silk White	$14.99		
Tomorrow's Not Promised – Robert Torres	$14.99		
Tomorrow's Not Promised 2 – Robert Torres	$14.99		
Two Mask One Heart – Jacob Spears and Trayvon Jackson	$14.99		
Two Mask One Heart 2 – Jacob Spears and Trayvon Jackson	$14.99		
Two Mask One Heart 3 – Jacob Spears and Trayvon Jackson	$14.99		
Wrong Place Wrong Time – Silk White	$14.99		
Young Goonz – Reality Way	$14.99		
Subtotal:			
Tax:			
Shipping (Free) U.S. Media Mail:			
Total:			

Make Checks Payable To:
Good2Go Publishing
7311 W Glass Lane,
Laveen, AZ 85339